THE MARK OF THE WOLF

GIACOMO GIAMMATTEO

Inferno Publishing Company

FOREWORD

Like all my books, this one is written in both third and first person. The headings showing a werewolf head will be in first person, and the ones showing a silver bullet will be in third person.

PROLOGUE

Arctic Wilderness - Early 1800s

Nukka took Atuat aside. "We need to hunt. The cellar has no meat, and you need a new coat for warmth."

"And you think the caribou will solve both problems?"

"They always have," Nukka said. "All we have to do is track them."

"Tracking them should be easy enough. A herd of caribou leave clear marks, marks that are easy to follow."

Nukka grabbed his spear. "Your coat is waiting."

The vast white expanse of the Arctic stretched endlessly under a gray winter sky. Nukka moved silently across the snow, following caribou tracks.

Atuat knelt beside a set of prints in the snow, studying them carefully. Her brow furrowed as she traced the outline with her mittened hand, and her breath formed clouds as she pulled her fur-lined hood tighter to keep out the fierce wind. "I see plenty of tracks, but no caribou."

Atuat's voice was barely audible above the howling wind, so she signaled Nukka to come closer. "These tracks not normal."

Nukka crouched beside her, examining several sets of prints more closely. He gripped his spear tighter, and the skin around his knuckles tightened under his sealskin gloves.

A blizzard raged around them, reducing visibility to a few feet, and snow whipped across their faces as they followed the tracks toward the coast.

Nukka stopped and pointed east, deeper into the storm. He waited for her to get closer. "Look. The tracks veer off sharply, and the stride is too long, like something frightened them badly and they are running from whatever it is."

She tugged on Nukka's arm and pointed to the shoreline. "A ship is wrecked, and stuck in the ice. It might be a fishing boat."

"We need to look. Men might need help."

Nukka and Atuat approached the ship cautiously, then went on deck. They took one step at a time, almost tiptoeing. Everything was eerily silent. "No one here," Atuat said.

"Not on deck, but we no check below yet."

Nukka continued walking and called loudly as he searched, but he got no response. "I'm going below," he yelled back to Atuat. "You stay here."

Nukka searched the sleeping quarters. He found blood splattered on the floor and walls. As he searched the storage areas, he found more blood — a lot more — but he found no signs of life. After a few moments, he trudged up the steps to the top deck.

Nukka walked to Atuat, shaking his head. "No one. I found lot of blood, but no trace of men."

"This is a white man's ship," Atuat said. "They can't survive in this weather."

"Then where are the bodies?" Nukka asked.

She pointed eastward. "They must look for shelter. We can find them if we hurry."

Nukka nodded, then he stepped off the ship, and soon spotted a set of tracks that appeared human. He signaled for Atuat to follow.

"Looks like at least one alive," Nukka said.

With Nukka holding his hunting spear, he and Atuat followed the tracks. The wind howled and the snow blinded them, restricting vision to a few feet. Eventually, the tracks led to a narrow mountain pass, and they entered cautiously. "Be careful," Nukka said. "Bears often hide from storms in passes like this."

As they advanced slowly, the wind carried strange sounds — not the normal Arctic wildlife, but something more menacing, more primal.

"You hear that?" Atuat asked.

"Must be bear. Big bear." Nukka gripped his spear tighter and held it shoulder-high.

As they got deeper into the pass, an image became clearer. They saw something that looked like a man, though his back was turned toward them. "That no bear," Atuat said.

Nukka nodded. "Looks like a man."

The man was wrapped in a full-length oilskin coat, and was taller than most.

Nukka called to him several times. "You hurt? Need help?" But the man never turned their way. As they drew closer, he slowly turned, and the full moon provided enough light for them to see the yellow eyes — it wasn't a man.

Atuat gasped, and froze, staring as it continued to turn. It had an elongated jaw and blood-stained teeth.

Nukka pushed Atuat back and told her to run as he raised his spear in a fighting stance. He planted. his feet and drew the spear back.

Atuat ran, but as she did, she heard a fierce, guttural growl. She turned to look, and saw that whatever it had been feasting on, it dropped, and it ran toward Nukka.

"Keep running," Nukka shouted.

He threw the spear sticking it in the beast's chest, but it didn't even slow it down. Nukka grabbed his second spear and jabbed at it as it came close.

The beast grabbed Nukka with its hand and slit his throat with long claws. He fell to the snow, his life's blood painting the snow red.

Atuat glanced over her shoulder as she ran, and she saw Nukka on the ground, still bleeding. And she saw whatever it was, coming for her.

It caught her easily, and attacked. Even worse, it passed along its curse — not through a bite, but through a violation that occurred in a way no woman wants.

Atuat's Village - Nine Months Later

Inside a small ice shelter, Atuat gave birth with the help of a village elder, Nayeli. She was a wise old woman who had helped many women give birth, and she knew all the legends.

A baby boy emerged, and Nayeli froze, then she slowly turned the baby toward Atuat. When Atuat saw the mark on the nape of the baby's neck, she gasped. It was dark, and in the shape of a crescent moon. It stood out against the baby's light-toned skin.

Nayeli's weathered face showed no emotion even though she recognized the mark from stories her grandmother told her. She held the baby, then gently wrapped it in a blanket and handed it to Atuat.

"Some say it is the mark of the Great Spirit, and that the boy will be blessed."

Then Nayeli's face grew grim. "Others say the mark is a curse brought by the white man traders."

She reached into a pouch she carried with her at all times, and handed Atuat an amulet. "This is made from walrus ivory, and it is meant to protect."

Atuat looked at the amulet. It was indeed pure ivory and it had the inlay of a white wolf with its head reared back as if howling.

Atuat pushed it away.

Nayeli face turned into a frown. "The amulet has protected generations, and some *angakkuit* (shamans) say if the mark is a curse, it might be broken with wisdom and compassion."

Atuat pursed her lips and stared. "No Great Spirit did this. It was the curse of the white man."

Nayeli handed the amulet back to her. "A good reason to keep the amulet."

Atuat held her son close, tears freezing on her cheeks as she realized the terrible legacy that now flowed through her bloodline. Outside, the wind howled, sounding like a wolf's cry, almost as if announcing the birth of something both blessed and damned.

Chapter One

A NEW BIRTH

Arviat Village, Alaska — Two Hundred Years Later

A small igloo sat on the edge of the village, positioned next to the beginning of the grazing plains, that extended for miles.

Nanook returned from a hunt, leading a sled pulled by his best dogs. A caribou sat on the back of the sled – food for months.

As Nanook neared the igloo, Siku waddled out to greet him, supporting her pregnant stomach as she walked. "Looks like you got lucky."

"Lucky? I am great warrior. At least, many people say I am. But I did get lucky. I got a caribou before wolves chase them away. If wolves get there first, caribou long gone."

Nanook patted her belly as he passed by her. "And how is boy today?"

Siku laughed, and followed him. "Could be girl."

Nanook shook his head, then led the dog sled into a small building outside the igloo. A door inside led down to an ice cellar, good for keeping meat for many months.

Nanook skinned the kill, then hung the meat in the cellar and went back up to Siku.

A small fire burned in the center of the floor, smoke rising through an opening at the top of the igloo, one that was covered with an animal skin when not needed.

Nanook sat close to the fire and rubbed his hands together. "Wife bring dinner?"

Siku brought him a bowl of soup filled with bones and organs for nourishment. "It good you make kill today. I have no more soup to give you."

Nanook smiled. "Good hunt today. Bring lots of food and fur to keep warm. Now I stay with you until boy come."

"Or girl."

Nanook laughed, then finished eating his soup. When he took the last sip, he stood to clean the bowl, but Siku got up quickly. "I get that, husband."

She took his bowl and headed toward the doorway, a small opening, more like a tunnel. It was made from carved blocks of ice.

She stooped down to get through, then grasped her stomach. "Nanook!"

Nanook rushed to her, picked her up and lay her on the bedding. "What do I do?"

"Get Kallik. She will know."

Nanook rushed to find the village mid-wife, and they soon returned to Siku.

Kallik immediately prepared Siku for delivery.

She turned to Nanook. "Make hot water, and get me towels and a knife. A sharp one."

"A knife?"

"I deliver many babies. We might need."

As Kallik worked on Siku, Nanook paced the igloo, and chewed his lower lip. He glanced to Siku every time he passed. Every time she moaned, he bit his lip harder.

After a moment, Siku moaned loudly, then shouted in pain. Suddenly, a baby's cry filled the igloo. Nanook rushed over to see Kallik holding a baby boy in her arms.

She smiled warmly and kissed the baby's forehead, then she handed him to Siku to hold. Nanook put blankets behind Siku's back, and she sat up, rocking the baby back and forth while she hummed.

Kallik patted the baby's bottom, then blew a kiss to Siku.

Kallik felt Siku's head, then announced she had to leave. "Must go quickly. Another baby tonight."

Nanook stepped forward. "Wait, Kallik. You must check the baby before you go."

"Not tonight. Maybe tomorrow."

Nanook nodded, then helped her out and quickly returned to Siku's side. "We have a boy, wife."

Siku held the baby up to Nanook. She kissed his head, then turned the baby around so that he faced Nanook.

"Look how strong," Nanook said. "He holds his head up high by himself."

As Nanook held the boy, Siku gasped and looked closer at the baby's neck.

"What wrong? Why you look like that?"

Siku took the baby in her hands, then turned him around so that his back faced Nanook. She pointed to the nape of his neck.

Nanook looked down and his eyes widened. He gasped. "No! Not our boy."

Nanook placed his thumb over the small mark on the baby's neck — a crescent moon. He tried brushing it off, but nothing happened. Nanook stared for a long time, then shook his head, tears running down his cheeks.

Siku sobbed. "What do we do?"

Nanook looked about nervously, as if someone were there. "We hide the mark. We have time."

The next day, Kallik returned. She examined the boy, who had a name now — Tulli. Her eyes turned stone cold when she saw the mark on his neck, then she reached into the pocket on her coat and produced an amulet. It was small, but detailed. Carved from walrus ivory, and depicting a white wolf with its head reared back, howling.

"Put this around his neck and never take it off. When he is old enough, make sure he understands he *must* wear this at all times. It may be the only thing that protects him."

Siku scoffed. "We already have amulet from long ago, but *nothing* will protect him from the white man's curse."

Siku looked to Nanook and saw him glaring. "But I will put it on him."

Chapter Two

HIS NAME IS TULLI

Three Years Later

I played in the snow with my friends, chasing each other and throwing snowballs, and laughing when one of us got hit. I scratched my neck continually, then removed my amulet and set it on a table sitting outside the house.

My mother rushed over and smacked the back of my head, then placed the amulet around my neck. She whispered as she clasped the amulet. "Never remove this. *Never.*"

I reluctantly put the amulet on, then continued playing with my friends and, all the while, wishing I didn't have to wear it.

One of the older boys hitched the dogs to the sled and drove them through the expanses of snow and ice, pretending to hunt like our fathers.

Four Years Later

I chased after Nanook as he rode away on the sled, off on a hunting trip.

"*Ataa!* (father) Wait for me."

Nanook turned his head, then halted the dogs. "Faster, Tulli."

I caught up to him and climbed onto the sled next to him. "We get *Anaana* (mother) a caribou for new coat? One that will keep her warm."

Nanook nodded, and we continued the hunt. We went after caribou twice, but the herd must have smelled us coming, and they ran off early. We couldn't catch them, not even with father's best dogs.

We rested while father fed the dogs. "Must give them energy, and let them rest."

After a short rest, we set out again. This time we caught a small herd by surprise, and father got two kills. One was a younger cow and the other, a mature bull. Both would provide good meat for many moons, and good fur to keep us warm.

The way back was against the wind all the way, and the wind had picked up tremendously. The snow blowing against our faces felt like little rocks, and the bitter cold penetrated our clothing and got under our skin. *I wish I hadn't come.*

Hours later, Nanook steered the sled next to our house. He entered, empty handed while I stayed outside.

Siku sat next to the small fire, her face showing disappointment when she saw Nanook empty-handed. "No luck, husband?"

Nanook smiled, then I walked in, carrying a freshly skinned and cleaned coat with soft fur.

I walked over and handed it to her, beaming. "For you, Anaana."

She hugged me and held me tightly. As she squeezed me close, she peeked behind my back. I could tell she was looking at the mark — it was more than a half-moon now. She pursed her lips and looked at Nanook, then turned to me. "Cut wood for fire."

I grabbed a hatchet and ran outside, knowing why she'd sent me. She wanted to talk to father without me being around.

Siku looked at Nanook. "You know what has to be done, husband. We can wait no more."

Nanook stomped his foot. "No! No sacrifice for Tulli."

Siku persisted. "People will see the mark when he bathes. They will demand sacrifice. And they will want to know why we do nothing. It goes against all village rules."

Nanook was adamant. "We move to a new village."

"He still needs to bathe," Siku said. "And what about when he goes to the springs? *Someone* will see the mark."

Nanook shook his head. "We go where people bathe inside."

Siku frowns. "I don't want to move again. I like it here."

Nanook's response is firm. "We go somewhere else, or I go alone."

He spread a map across the table, and his finger traced routes south. The lines on his face spoke of too many moves and too many fresh starts. He looked at Siku, who tended to a wound on her arm.

"We go south, to Oregon. The old ways are not so strong there. Maybe we find peace."

Siku nodded "Maybe."

Oregon, Ten Years Later

We got settled in Oregon and built a new life. Before long, I made new friends, and soon got into school activities. I even got into some sports.

I wanted to join the swim team, but that would have meant exposing the nape of my neck, which I had no desire to do. A few years later though, I joined the basketball team. Before games or practices, I made sure to cover up my neck — sometimes using bandages and sometimes makeup to cover the mark. It worked well unless someone were to closely inspect it.

I was playing basketball in the gym, went for a jump shot, and got knocked to the floor. In the scramble to get up, my bandage came off, and one of the team saw the birthmark on my neck.

He wasted no time in ribbing me about it. "Hey, guys, look at this. Tulli's got a full moon birthmark on his neck."

I decided the best way out of the situation was to deflect the comment with one of my own. I adopted a well-practiced grin. "It's a family birthmark, asshole. My people call it the mark of the wolf."

I reached for my friend who saw the mark and bared my teeth. "That means I turn into a werewolf under the full moon."

Everyone laughed, including myself, but my smile didn't reach my eyes.

We played another game, then we showered and I went home.

When I got home, I went to my room and stared at a map I had hanging on the wall. Red Xs marked the towns where I'd lived: four in Alaska — that I could remember — and now Oregon. *And I can't remember a friend from any of them.*

I fingered the amulet around my neck, then checked a lunar chart, showing phases of the moon. I traced the calendar to see when a full moon would occur, but it wasn't until the next night. That left me enough time. I had an urge to be with people.

As I prepared to leave the house, I checked again to make sure the moon wasn't full, then I took a long drive into the mountains, ending up at a remote, rough-hewn tavern called "Timbers".

The bar sat isolated among thick woods, with snow-capped mountains looming in the background. Inside, the atmosphere was rough and unwelcoming. Local loggers and hunters nursed their drinks while country music blared from a jukebox in the corner.

I ordered a beer and tried to blend into the shadows, but my short-lived peace was shattered when three lumberjacks burst through the door.

The first man, burly with calloused hands, walked over to a corner table where a young woman sat alone. He rested his palms on the table and leaned in close.

He was loud enough to hear even above the music. "You been waitin' for me, sweetie?"

She shifted in her seat, obviously uncomfortable.

I ordered two beers and went to her table, then I handed her a beer and sat across from her. "Sorry it took me so long to get this. The bartender was swamped."

The man scoffed. "This is the guy you're with? He ain't half a man. "

He jabbed his finger in my chest. "And you shouldn't be leaving such a pretty girl by herself."

Then he reached down and grabbed my amulet. "Look, he wears a necklace. "

A few of the patrons laughed. Some hooted and hollered, riling him up more.

An image of my dad giving me the amulet flashed in my mind. I clenched my fist around the amulet tightly and stood up. I felt my body changing, and when I spoke, my voice was deeper than normal, and gravelly. "You need to let go of the amulet."

"Or what?" the man asked.

I focused on his eyes. "I make you."

The man swung at me, but I stepped aside, then pummeled him

with two jabs and a right hook, knocking him to the floor. I grabbed him as he fell, then twisted the man's arm until it broke.

He wiped blood from his lip as he stood, his arm limp at his side. "Don't like your necklace touched, huh, boy?"

He pulled a knife from his pocket, positioned himself in a fighting stance, and approached slowly. "Now, I'm gonna have to take it."

He feinted a jab with the knife, then lunged at me. I caught his fist in mid-air and pressured him to the floor.

Both the other men moved to attack me. I kicked the second man on the side of the leg, snapping it. The third man swung a bottle at me, but I blocked it with my arm.

The bottle broke making a large gash on my forearm, but I didn't stop. I grabbed him, the tips of my fingers now small, sharp claws. I was about to snap his neck, but then I noticed the fear in several patron's eyes.

I let go, but my claws dug gashes into the man's chest. When I saw the blood, I dropped him to the floor.

I walked over and stretched my hand out to the young woman. "Come with me. I'll see you home safely."

As I left with the young woman the other patrons mumbled under their breaths. "Beast. Monster. Freak."

Once outside, the woman got into her car and cranked the engine.

"Do you need a ride home?" I asked.

The young woman appeared frightened. She rolled up her window and stammered out a reply. "I'm f-fine now. Thank you."

I watched her leave, then examined my bloodstained knuckles and noticed my muscles seemed unnaturally prominent.

I watched her go, then realized it was time to leave — again.

I drove until I found a phone booth on the side of the road. Idaho was one of those that still had phone booths. I got out and dialed a familiar number, praying for an answer.

An old feeble voice answered. "Hello?"

"Aanak (grandmother), it's Tulli."

"Tulli! So nice to hear your voice. "

A moment of silence, then: "It's happened again, Aanak."

Aanak said nothing for a moment, then she asked. "How bad?"

"I hurt people. Three of them."

Aanak sighed. "You know what you have to do. You can't stay there. Do you still have the amulet?"

"Always, Aanak."

"Trust in it. It might not seem like it, but it will help. It carries the power of the Great Wolf Spirit."

As I drove, memories of my father, Nanook, flashed through my mind.

Chapter Three

IT'S TIME TO LEAVE – AGAIN

I got home late, real late, and tried to be quiet as I entered the house, not wanting to wake my father or mother. I knew they'd be sleeping.

As I crept toward the stairs I heard my father's voice, though it was barely above a whisper. "You've been out late, son?"

I hung my head low. "I know. I was just riding, then walking."

"Sit down, and tell me what makes my son drive and walk instead of sleep."

I slumped into a chair and began my story, telling him everything that happened at the bar. "Then I called Aanak, and she said I had to leave before they found me."

Nanook smiled. "She is always right. When I was young, I often thought she was wrong, but time proved she wasn't."

Nanook got up and hugged me for a long time. I felt his tears drop on my neck, which made me cry too.

He then stepped back and spoke in his fatherly advice voice. "Remember — the night before a full moon, the wolf inside you begins to shift. The body grows stronger, but the mind grows weaker, and evil creeps in."

He paused and took a few breaths. "But the heart remains strong." He stared. "If your heart is true, you will be fine."

I nodded.

Nanook stopped me as I walked across the room. "Always keep your amulet. The Great Spirit will protect you, and if you show compassion and wisdom, the curse will be lifted."

"When?"

Nanook bowed his head. "Someday."

"Ataata, what if I'm about to change when I don't want to?"

Nanook moved feebly now, but he got up and reached for a small box sitting on the top shelf next to the window. "Take this silver necklace. It will hurt you, like any silver, but it may keep you from changing when you don't want to."

Nanook looked at me and smiled. "It was passed down from my great grandfather, who had the curse like you, but he learned to control it. And he lived a long life."

The floor creaking caused my father to turn his head; it was my mother entering the room. Her face was unreadable, but her words were *very* understandable. "You must go," she said. "There is no place for you here."

"I don't want to go. Not again. I finally have a home."

Nanook looks out the window. "You can't leave now anyway. The moon will soon be full."

I shrugged, then opened the door and walked to the cellar. In the corner was a small cell with a sink and a toilet. Nanook, following me, waited for me to get inside, then locked the door, and took the keys with him. "We bring food later."

Nanook left me shivering. All I could do was stare out the window and wait. As darkness settled, I saw the moon, round and full. I knew what was coming, and I wasn't excited.

The transformation began with sudden pain as bones cracked and reshaped. My fingers extended into claws and my face elongated into a muzzle filled with sharp teeth.

Coarse hair covered my body and my posture changed to a more animal-like form. I smelled the food when Nanook brought it down the stairs, and the hunger within me produced a primal howl, that completed the change.

Nanook stood at the top of the steps, listening. When I howled,

Nanook wiped a tear from his eye, and opened the door.

In the morning, Nanook opened the cell door, hugging me as I came out.

"Thank you, Ataa."

I helped Nanook up the last few steps, and into the kitchen. Nanook held his chest as he walked.

Exhausted, I sat at the table, hoping for a warm cup of tea, which I asked for; instead, my mother sat still, sipping her tea and ignoring my request.

She turned to Nanook. "How long you keep this up?"

Nanook shuffled his feet as he moved across the floor. "As long as I live — maybe not so long."

Siku moved to the stove and scooped food onto a plate, then she took it to the table and set it before Nanook. "I no keep him. When you go, he go."

"He's your son. Why you say such things?"

Siku glares and jams her finger into Nanook's chest. "You know why. My brother never saw ten. Never had a girlfriend. All because of werewolf. I won't have him do that to another family."

Nanook breathed heavily. "Tulli, take me to bed."

I helped him to bed, then covered him with blankets.

Siku walked in. "I call doctor. He be here soon."

Nanook pulled me closer, and whispered.

"You must go far away. Start a new life. Your mother not strong enough to keep you." He took a few deep breaths. "But always remember — you no hurt innocent people."

Nanook reached out and held my hands. "And remember, you have curse and gift. Learn. Be wise."

I nodded, tears in my eyes.

"Be strong-minded. Have strength. Be resilient," Nanook said.

I nodded. "I promise." I held Nanook until his head fell to the side, then I cried.

Siku sobbed uncontrollably, and banged her fists on the table.

I walked to her side and held her. She squeezed me tightly, then looked at Nanook, lying still on the bed.

"I can no protect you like your Atta. You must go. Now."

I looked on in disbelief but then I packed my belongings and prepared to leave.

My mother kissed me goodbye. "You know I love my boy, but I can't let you stay."

I nodded and walked out the door carrying a backpack stuffed with clothes and a hunting knife from Nanook. I turned before leaving and saw my mother standing there, staring. "Goodbye Anaana. I'll miss you."

Chapter Four

LOOKING FOR A HOME

I walked along the snow-covered road and stopped at every small store or gas station so I could warm my feet and hands. I took as long as I could, pretending to shop, or inching close to a heater if they had one. Usually the owners chased me out of the store before I got comfortable, and I had to continue my trek, keeping my hands in my pocket except for when a car drove by and I pulled my right hand out to hitchhike. It said a lot about people that they drove by without offering a ride, especially on a day as cold as this.

Two cars in a row passed me by, not even slowing. When a third one passed, I muttered. *I don't know why I couldn't stay at home.*

I didn't know where I was though I knew I was still in Oregon because I hadn't seen a sign that read 'Welcome to Idaho.'

Before long, I saw a gas station and went inside to get warm. Once inside, I noticed a job posting on a board. It was a local lumber mill looking for workers.

I turned to the owner. "You know if they're still looking?"

He nodded. "As of yesterday, they were."

"Where are they?" I asked.

"Keep going down this road, and you'll come up on them. Maybe a mile. Maybe two."

"Okay, thanks." I almost ran out the door and walked at a fast pace down the road. *I've got to get there before someone takes that job.*

Half an hour later, I saw a sign for Woody's Lumber Mill. I went inside and asked to speak to the owner.

"You still looking for workers?"

"Hard workers only."

"That's me," I said. "I can start whenever you want."

He looked me over, then nodded. "Be here tomorrow at 7:00. If you last the week, you're hired."

I left the mill with a smile and the few belongings I had, then I set out to look for a place to stay. I had no money, so I headed into the woods to find a place to pitch a tent, somewhere remote. A few miles into the woods, I found a small clearing. It was surrounded by dense forest, and would allow me to build a fire to keep warm and to cook. It also allowed me to sleep in peace.

After my first day of work, I borrowed enough money for food and coffee, then went back to my tent, and, for the first time in days, had a meal that kept my stomach from growling.

I settled in early, intent on getting sleep, but the incessant howling of coyotes ensured that didn't happen.

After the first week, the boss smiled and welcomed me as a worker — a full-time worker. He paid me for the week, minus the loan he'd made me, then said I'd be making more per hour now that I was full time.

The money gave me enough to stop at the store and buy a good supply of food and coffee, then I went 'home' and cooked my first meal with meat in a long time.

I was getting accustomed to my new routine, but when I came home a few nights later, I found my camp had been raided by what appeared to have been bears, and they'd been thorough. They ransacked my food supply, though at least they left me with coffee.

That night, while warming myself by the fire, I felt the change beginning. I looked up and saw the moon was full, so I ran as fast as I could, deeper into the forest and farther from civilization. When I reached a spot I felt was remote enough, I sat down and let the change happen. The change was painful, always was, but at least I was far enough away so I wouldn't hurt anyone.

Weeks later, I had saved enough money to buy a used pickup. I had no rent, water, electricity, or taxes, to pay — nothing but food, which made it easy to save.

It made life easier having wheels, allowing me to sleep in longer and drive to work instead of walking, and using the truck to shop for food and bring it home.

Things were going fine for a while, and I was getting used to my lifestyle, then springtime came and more and more campers arrived.

That night, I fell into a deep sleep but the sound of an owl hooting woke me. I almost leapt from my bed, clutching the amulet that is always around my neck. I cautiously looked outside the tent, but saw nothing out of order, so I once again rested my head on the pillow and closed my eyes.

In the morning, I realized what probably caused the owls to hoot; the immediate area was heavily populated with new campsites.

As I built a fire to make coffee, one of the campers approached. "Been here long?"

"A little while," I said.

"I kinda like it here," he said. "Nice and quiet."

"I guess so, but I'm not staying long. Hope you enjoy your time here."

I packed up my things and put them in the truck. Most of them fit into a small metal box one of the guys at the mill made me; the rest, I put in the cab.

After enjoying my coffee, I headed off to work.

I turned in my notice when I got in, and Woody said to expect a good recommendation. He said for anyone who asks, tell them to call Woodrow, not Woody.

After work, I found a small motel that had a room that I could rent until I left, so I checked in there, hoping for a few nights of good sleep.

Chapter Five

A NEW HOME

I headed east, looking for someplace that I could settle down. I tried out a few towns, but nothing worked, so I kept moving on.

Shortly after crossing the Idaho border, I came upon Valley's End, a small town that appeared to have vibrant businesses, catering to not only other small towns, but the nearby ski resorts as well.

I parked my truck near the end of the town's main street and strolled along a wood-planked walkway in front of an impressive stream of stores.

About halfway down, I came upon Little Hawk, an older Native American sitting in a rocking chair in front of a store touting baskets, blankets, and other handmade items. The windows had strings of beads hanging down from various items attached to the walls or ceiling.

"New in town?" Little Hawk asked.

I nodded. "I just got in, and I'm looking for work, so if you know any —"

Little Hawk pointed east. "Half a mile that way is Jasper's lumber mill. He always needs hard workers."

I took Little Hawk's advice and went to see Jasper.

. . .

"Ever worked at a mill?" Jasper asked.

"Two years experience, over in Oregon. Woody's Lumber Mill. It's near —"

Jasper nodded. "I know Woody. If he gives you a good reference, you're as good as hired." He looked me up and down, then asked. "What kind of work did he have you doing?"

"I started as a mill worker, then moved to running a planer, then to sawmill machine operator. After a while on the sawmill, Woody had me train as a millwright, but I left before I got certified."

"Why'd you leave? I know Woody, and he's a good guy."

I lowered my head. I hated to start a relationship with a lie, but there wasn't much I could do; besides, this wasn't a real lie. "My dad died, leaving my mother alone. Somebody had to help her."

Jasper nodded. "Woody will back up your story, I guess."

I reached in my wallet and pulled out a crumpled piece of paper. "His number's right here. He said if I needed a reference, to call this number and ask for Woodrow."

Jasper laughed. "All right, boy. You're hired, and as a millwright."

"Aren't you gonna call Woody?"

"No need. Me and Woody got a code. If you said call "Woody," I'd have known you were full of shit, but call "Woodrow" means you're the real deal. I do the same only I tell them to ask for Jasper D."

"Thank you, Jasper. Thanks so much."

"How much did Woody pay you?"

I looked at Jasper and gulped. "I was getting $39 an hour, but I know that might be high. I'd be willing —"

"That's high, but I'm not one that would ask a good man to work for less. Consider your pay to be $39.00 per hour, presuming you live up to Woodrow's word."

I smiled. "You can count on it, sir." I turned to leave, then turned back. "One thing, sir. Once a month I need to check on my mother. I'm never sure which day, but it'd be about once a month. I'll be happy to work any other day to make up for it though."

"Good enough. See you in the morning."

"I'll be here at seven sharp."

"You'll be an hour early, but whatever suits you."

I laughed. "Then I'll be here at eight."

Jasper smiled. "That'll work fine. See you then."

After work the next day, I went to explore more of the town. I waved to Little Hawk as I walked by. "Hey, Little Hawk. I Got that job. Thanks."

Little Hawk nodded and continued rocking in his chair.

I passed a few more shops, then saw two young girls standing by the side of the street. I walked up to them, and leaned down to their level. "You two lost? Or need help?"

The shorter one held out her hand to shake. "I'm Linda. We're just waiting on my mom to pick us up. She's always late."

"I can walk you home if you want. My name's Tulli."

"Hi, Tulli. This is my friend, Amy." Linda pointed behind me. "And that's my big sister Celie."

A beautiful young woman walked up and smiled at me, then she reached to shake my hand. "You must be new here. I know most people in town."

"I'm thinking of settling down here. Just looking for a place to stay."

"My mom's renting a room. Wanna look at it."

I hesitated. It sounded good, and I felt an attraction to this girl, but my personal situation would make it unworkable. "I don't know. How close are you to town, and to the lumber mill? I just got a job there."

Celie looked disappointed. "We're the opposite way from the mill, but old man Billings is renting his cabin about half a mile north of the mill. It's kind of remote though."

I know my face lit up; I could feel it. "That sounds like it might be ideal."

"If you're interested, talk to Little Hawk. He'll put you in touch with old man Billings."

Before I could even thank her, Linda's mother pulled up and gave them all a ride home.

I talked to Little Hawk, got directions for where to find Billings, then got in my truck and drove to see him. Billings and I then rode to the cabin. It only took minutes to negotiate a deal, and Billings said I could move in immediately.

After Billings left, I stepped outside and looked around. It was truly perfect: isolated, and inexpensive.

I unpacked my belongings and settled in. For the first time in years, I felt as if I had a home. I cracked open a can of fruit cocktail, opened a bag of chips, then grabbed a map I keep in a chest and spread it across the table.

I located Valley's End, and drew a circle around it in green. *This is going to be home.*

As I settled into the cabin, I thought of Nanook. I had such good memories of him, worthwhile ones too, like when he gave me the silver necklace; and him reminding me of the power of the amulet, and not to take it off. And most importantly, when he told me that my powers could be used for good. I wanted so badly for that to be true.

Chapter Six

THE DANCE

As Celie came down the stairs, her brother, Clark, threw a tennis ball at his younger sister Linda's, causing her to chase him through the house. As they raced through the kitchen, Rita, their mother, placed her hands on her hips and glared. "Enough of this. Clean up and get ready for dinner."

Celie stepped in and lent a hand, helping her mother prepare dinner.

"Who was the young man I saw you with?" Rita asked.

Celie smiled. "He's new in town. His name's Tulli."

"I think Celie likes him," Linda said.

Rita stirred the gravy and sprinkled in flour while adding pepper. "He looks a little old for you, dear. Maybe you shouldn't see him."

Celie rolled her eyes. "Mom, all I did was walk with him."

"I know, but he seems ... off."

"So I can only date boys that you like?"

"I didn't say that."

Celie tossed a dishtowel on the counter. "I hope not because you didn't fare so well with the men you chose. Dad stayed around a while, but you said yourself that he was a loser. And the guy you dated after him was worse."

"That's enough out of you, young lady. Get the table set."

Sheila Litkin, Amy's mother, tossed a thick jacket to Josh as he prepared to leave. "Where do you think you're going?"

Josh caught the jacket, put it on, and zippered it up. "Out with Clark. Maybe going to the dance with Donna and Henry."

"The school dance?"

"No, the town hall dance. That's where everybody goes."

Just outside of town, I took a shortcut toward the cabin. It was an old lumber trail that winded through the woods. Just as I started up the hill, Celie called to me.

"Tulli! Wait up."

She walked quickly to my side. "Where are you going?"

"On my way home. I rented that house you recommended, but I've still got a lot to clean up."

Celie twisted her hair in curls and flashed a smile. "Aren't you going to the dance tonight? I don't have a date, if you want to go with me."

I beamed, but then looked upward. *The moon is almost full.* "Damn, Celie, I can't tonight, but I'd love to another time."

"If you're worried about fitting in, don't. There are plenty of Native Americans here from —"

"It's not that, but thanks."

Celie lowered her head and frowned. "Oh, okay. Another time then."

As she walked away, she muttered to herself. "It's Friday night. What's he doing that's so important?"

I watched her go, shoulders slumped, head lowered, so I ran to catch up, then grabbed her and turned her around. "I'm sorry, Celie. I just can't make it tonight, but the next one for sure."

I leaned close to her, my lips only inches from hers. Her breath was hot on my face as I kissed her. "I promise, we'll go soon."

Donna Litkin applied her makeup, put on her lipstick, and then her coat.

Henry, Donna's older brother and a well-built jock, moved briskly through the room. "Don't tell me you're going to the dance, sis."

Donna glared at Henry as he rushed toward the front door. "Of course, I'm going. Isn't everybody? So cut the crap, Henry. And you better wait for me. I'm not walking through those woods by myself — especially not at night."

Henry stopped at the door. "Hurry the hell up then. You too, Little Pup. I assume you're going."

"I'm ready. Just waiting on Donna — as usual."

. . .

The woods were thick and the night was dark, save for the light when the full moon shone through breaks in the trees. As they walked through the woods, Henry set a fast pace, one that Donna and Josh couldn't keep up with.

Donna yelled as she fell behind. "Slow down, for God's sake."

Josh picked up a small stone and threw it at Henry, hitting him in the back. "Slow down, asshole; it's your sister back here."

Henry came to a stop, turned around, and grabbed hold of Donna's hand. "Come on, sis. I'll keep you with me until we get there."

He then turned and smiled while he shot Josh the finger. "You too, baby brother. I'll even keep your ass safe." Henry lifted his jacket to show a gun tucked in his waistband. "Nobody's gonna mess with me."

"Oh, God, Henry. Do you always carry that gun, or are you just trying to be like Dad?"

* * *

At the entrance to the town hall, an attendant collected tickets and tore them in half to allow admittance. The line to get in lengthened, but Henry nudged his way in.

When they collected Henry's ticket, he turned and tapped Donna on the shoulder. "Don't bother me until the dance is over."

He pointed at Josh, who was waiting in line behind Donna. "And tell that little puppy to leave me alone."

Celie's brother Clark ran up to Josh. He was breathing hard. "Are we going inside?"

Josh shrugged. "I guess so. Donna's in there. And Henry."

Clark paid for his ticket and followed Josh inside. Henry connected with Liane, his old girlfriend — and danced across the floor with her to every song.

As Henry and Liane danced past Donna and her suitor, Henry reached out and tapped her shoulder. "Tell the puppy that I'm leaving as soon as the last song plays, so he better be ready. I don't want to get stuck in the crowd."

Donna decided to leave early so Henry didn't have to wait. She sat on the porch with Josh and Clark.

When Henry finally showed, he had Liane, his old girlfriend, with him. He nodded to Donna and led them down the steps and off the porch. "I'm glad to see you left on time. C'mon, follow me closely."

They crossed the street, then walked along a narrow path through the woods. About one hundred yards in, Liane turned onto another trail. "This way. It's a shortcut."

"Shortcut to what?" Josh asked. "It's black as pitch and no one's gonna hear us if we scream."

Liane sneered. "If you want to get home quicker, follow me. Or, you can find your own way."

Donna shrugged and looked at Josh. "I'm going with them."

Josh shook his head, but then Clark tugged on his sleeve. "I don't want to go that way."

Josh looked ahead to Henry, then back to Clark. "C'mon, scaredy cat. What are you afraid of?"

Clark looked back toward town, then ahead up the dark path. Finally, he shrugged and moved forward. "All right. Let's go."

As they moved farther down the path, sounds from the woods followed them, almost like a rustling of leaves. Clark and Josh ran up to be near Henry, and for a moment seemed at ease.

Then, from behind them, the sound of a deep guttural growl came from the darkest part of the woods.

Donna panicked. "Did you hear that?"

Josh turned his head toward the sound, but he tried to brush it off. "I didn't hear anything."

All of them huddled closer together and increased their pace, almost running. They turned their heads side to side, none of them saying a word. Then Donna spoke up. "That sounds like a growl, a deep growl."

After fifty or sixty feet, Henry stopped and got behind a tree. He pulled a gun from his waistband, and held it up for all to see. His eyes showed grim determination. "Go home and get Dad. Run, and don't look back. I'll be there before you know it."

* * *

Liane, Donna, and the boys ran toward the house, leaving Henry behind. He stood with the tree in front of him, and held his gun at his side.

He heard a slight rustling noise again, then tilted his head from side to side, listening closer. A growl from the left caught his attention, but when he looked to see what it was, something grabbed him, and yanked him out from behind the tree.

It slashed his face with long claws, then disappeared deep into the woods. Henry lay on the ground, blood pooling under him, oozing from his wounds.

* * *

Donna and the others raced out of the woods and up the steps at the Litkin home, stopping for nothing. They ran across the porch, and pushed open the front door. "Dad! Dad, something's after us."

Ellis Litkin walked in from the kitchen, almost laughing. "Hold up. Hold up. What's after you?"

He looked around, puzzled. "And where's Henry?"

Josh was almost in tears. "That's what we're trying to tell you, Dad. We were on the way home and heard growling. Henry stayed behind to protect us."

A concerned look appeared on Ellis's face. He grabbed his shotgun and rushed for the door. "Stay here. Nobody goes out. And lock the door."

Chapter Seven

THE INCIDENT

Ellis ran down the narrow trail, loading his gun as he went, and he didn't stop running until he got to a clearing that appeared all torn up: branches broken, and leaves ripped from limbs.

He looked about, then turned on his flashlight and looked some more. On the far side, lay a shredded body.

A sick feeling tore at his gut, and when he investigated, he discovered it was Henry.

He lowered himself and pounded on the body, crying and moaning as he did. "No. No! Goddamn, no."

He knelt on the ground and cradled Henry's head in his hands. then lay Henry's head on his lap. "Why?"

After gaining some composure, Ellis called Mollie, the local sheriff, and though barely able to talk, he got out the words. "Mollie, my boy. My boy ..."

"Ellis? Is that you?"

"I'm on the trail by where the train crosses over the creek." Ellis sobbed, and choked on his words. "It's Henry. He's dead."

"Oh, my God. I'm on my way."

. . .

Mollie pulled up the trail and parked on the side. She left her headlights on.

Up ahead, Ellis walked in circles, shotgun in hand. His arms and face were covered in blood — Henry's blood. His knees collapsed as Mollie grew closer.

Mollie rushed up the trail. "Jesus, Ellis, are you okay?"

"It's my boy, Mollie. It's Henry."

Mollie looked down at the body, then turned away. "I'm so sorry, Ellis. I don't know what to say."

Ellis nodded and did his best to stand, but he stumbled. "I need to know who did this. "

Once he got his feet, he reached out to touch Henry's body again, but fell. "I'm sorry, Henry."

Mollie patted his back and knelt beside him. "Let's get you home so you can rest. I'll take care of your boy."

Mollie helped Ellis into the backseat of her car, then called her deputy. "Get up here as soon as you can and take command of the investigation. And pay attention to details; this is Ellis Litkin's son."

"Yes, ma'am. I'll get it done."

Mollie drove Ellis home and let him off by the front steps. "You need me to come in?"

Ellis shook his head. "I'm all right, but thanks."

Ellis trudged up the steps and into the house. His wife, Sheila, greeted him, then he turned to embrace Josh, Donna, and Amy.

Donna, with worry on her face, hugged him the longest. "Dad, are you all right? Did you find Henry?"

Ellis plopped onto the sofa and put his elbows on his knees, then he buried his head in his hands and cried. "I was too late. He's gone. Henry's gone."

He cried some more. "I should have taught him to shoot better."

Sheila ran over and knelt in front of Ellis. She grabbed his head and shook it. "What do you mean, 'he's gone?' "

"He's dead, Sheila. Dead!"

"How? Where? What happened?"

Ellis shook his head more and sobbed louder. "I don't know."

Donna rested her head on Josh's shoulder and cried. "We shouldn't have let him stay by himself. "

Sheila did her best to compose herself. "You couldn't have done anything, dear. Henry was your older brother, and regardless of what you said, he'd have stayed behind to protect you."

Donna shrugged. "I guess."

Amy and Josh ran to their rooms, crying, and Sheila sobbed uncontrollably, then moved back to Ellis.

"We'll get whoever did this. I swear."

Sheila continued to cry, but offered a voice of reason. "Let's deal with this tomorrow. There's nothing we can do tonight."

Sheila brought coffee to the table and bent down to kiss Ellis good morning. He turned his cheek.

"Did you sleep?" she asked.

Ellis snapped at her. "What do you think?"

He pushed his coffee aside. "I'm going to town, and see if Mollie has any news."

At the sheriff's office, Ellis waited in line behind two others to see the officer at the front desk. After a moment, he pushed them aside. "Here to see Sheriff Newsom. She knows I'm coming."

Mollie stepped out of her office. "In here, Ellis."

Mollie put her hands on her desk and stared. "I normally ask if you knew anyone who'd want to harm the deceased, but this is different. It looks like it was an animal of some kind that did this."

Ellis said nothing, causing Mollie to speak again. "You can have another look, but I've also got pictures."

Ellis nodded and turned his head. "No need to see the body, or the pictures. I saw too much last night."

Mollie gestured to a tech, indicating he clean up the body, then she escorted Ellis outside.

Mollie and Ellis exited the back door, then walked across the parking lot and into a small refrigerated building that looked like a small barn.

Mollie opened the padlock and swung the door open, then she stepped aside to let Ellis enter. As they walked toward the back, Mollie gestured to the refrigerated compartments that lined both side walls.

"What are we doing here?" Ellis asked.

"We use this for anything that needs to be kept cold, and that includes bodies."

Mollie looked to Ellis and continued. "The doctor only gets down here every week or so, and she likes the bodies kept neat and clean."

"That's all good, Mollie, but what am *I* doing here? "

"I want you to look at a body that was brought in a few days ago. They found it in Tyson's Creek about six miles from here."

Mollie noted the sour look on Ellis's face, but she went on. "I know you're not a doctor, but you've seen more claw marks than most, so I figured it wouldn't hurt for you to take a peek."

Ellis looked around at the sterile environment. He smelled nothing, but saw his breath freeze as he spoke. He turned to Mollie and stammered. "I don't know if I want to see it, Mollie. Not now."

Mollie nodded. "I understand. Maybe another time."

Ellis began to walk away, but turned back to Mollie. "Aw hell. If you think it could help, I'll take a look."

Mollie nodded again, then opened the door and flipped on the light switch. She entered a large empty section of the warehouse with a line of five tables in the center. Everything was scrubbed clean, and a body lay on the first table.

She walked to the body and removed the plastic cover.

After Ellis moved alongside her, she pointed to the neck. "See what you think of these compared to the marks on Henry."

Ellis pulled aside the cover and removed a few bandages. He pulled back quickly, his face contorted in pain.

"I'm sorry, Ellis."

"It's all right. I'm okay."

He then rolled the body over to inspect closer. "Without them being side by side, I can't swear, but this looks more than similar to Henry's — it's damn near identical."

Mollie nods as she covers the body. "That's what I thought too, and I can't see two such things happening so close together."

Mollie holds Ellis's hand. "You need to take a minute?"

Ellis shook his head. "What are you gonna do?"

"I'll see if I can get help. But until they get here, I might need to call on you for one thing or another. You up for it?"

"I'll be home except when we put my boy in the ground. All I want to do is catch the son of a bitch who did this."

Ellis scanned his library of books and selected a half a dozen of them.

"What are you looking for?"

"I'm lookin' into some things that might help with Henry."

Sheila bent over and shouted. "Help with Henry? He's dead!"

A knock sounded at the door, and Sheila answered. It's Mollie. "I've got another boy up in Mill's run, Ellis."

"Like Henry?"

"I don't know. All I know is I'm sick of lookin' at dead bodies."

Mollie lowered her head. "I'm sure you are too, but I'm asking if you want to join me."

Ellis put the glasses in a sink piled with dirty dishes. Then he called to Sheila. "I'm going with Mollie. We shouldn't be too long."

Chapter Eight

ANOTHER BODY

Ellis settled into the center seat at the head table, and Mollie took the seat next to him. She leaned over and whispered. "Let the townsfolk start the discussion, but chime in whenever you feel the need to."

Ellis and Mollie chatted while people walked in and filled the seats, each with a mug of beer on the table before them.

The blacksmith gulped the rest of his beer and refilled it from a pitcher to his side, then he slammed his fist on the table, drawing everyone's attention. "We gonna talk about what happened or just sit around and gab?"

Ellis shouted. "We're gonna talk." He looked out over the crowd. "Anybody have an idea who did this?"

The blacksmith was adamant. "Ain't no *who* about it. I seen lots of wolf bites, and I say it was a wolf. Maybe even two of 'em."

Ellis banged a gavel on the table until the crowd settled down. Once they were quiet, he spoke. "This was no wolf. And it wasn't a bear, or coyotes, or cougars. I don't know what it was, but it wasn't any of them."

Mollie shouted to get attention. "You need to listen to Ellis. He's a guide for them damn weekend hunters that come up here, and he's seen more than his fair share of claw marks on animals and humans both."

Bushcat, a middle-aged Native American, smacks the table top. "I say it's a werewolf. Some say they're myths, but I'm not sure. My people believe in them."

Little Hawk stood up and addressed the crowd. He spoke slowly and somberly. "Most of you aren't old enough to remember the massacres at Running Creek or Bear Ridge, but they were brutal. Men, women, and children mangled, and no one was caught. They blamed an animal. But it wasn't just any animal."

The blacksmith called out. "What was it?"

Little Hawk waited for the noise to settle down before speaking. "My people have been hunting these grounds for thousands of years. Wolf god not evil. But once every hundred years or more, a wolf spirit turns bad. It takes human form and is born with The mark of the wolf — a crescent moon that grows every year. When moon is full, boy becomes werewolf."

Mollie, frustrated at the turn of events, addresses Little Hawk. "Little Hawk, you're not even from this town. Why are you here?"

Grant Williams, a loud-mouthed drunk, tries to stand but falls back into his seat. "And the only way to kill them is with a silver bullet," he said, though the slurring of his words made it difficult to understand him.

Nonetheless, enough of the crowd understood him, and they yelled all at once. "Melt down your silver to make bullets or knives."

"I've got my silver arrow heads," yelled Bushcat.

The blacksmith stood and banged on the table. "Melt down your silver to make bullets or knives. I've got my silver arrow heads."

Ellis, sensing things had gotten out of hand, banged the gavel, then reached down and grabbed Mollie's hand. "I think it's time we go."

Mollie and Ellis head back to Valley's End. She slowed down as they approached a series of deadly curves running above a ravine, and turned to Ellis. "What did you think?"

Ellis looked out the window and stared at a deep gorge. "Keep your eyes on the road, and I'll tell you."

Mollie gripped the steering wheel tightly, and formed a rigid look as she stared straight ahead. "I'm listening."

"Little Hawk said interesting things."

Mollie chuckled. "Little Hawk always has interesting things to say. Most of them are nonsense, but they're interesting."

Ellis looked over at Mollie. "Did you get anything out of the meeting?"

"Nothing much. I got that most people would rather believe in myths than search for the truth."

"I say we forget about the myths and stick to the evidence. It'll point us to who killed Henry."

"That's a good plan, Ellis."

Mollie pulled up to Ellis' house, and he got out, then he leaned on the car door and stuck his head inside. "If we mention 'werewolf' to anyone, it will stir things up with the locals."

"I know, and I have no intention of saying anything. And, Ellis, try to be at the office by nine."

Mollie started to pull away, but then stopped and rolled the window down. She leaned over and hollered. "And bring some good ideas."

～

Donna and Josh mob Ellis when he entered. "What happened, Dad?" Donna asked.

"Did the sheriff tell you anything?" Josh asked.

Ellis shook his head. "I know this is crazy, but they're talking like it's a werewolf." Ellis held up his hands to calm them. "But don't worry, Mollie's calling the FBI up in Couer d'Alene tomorrow. They'll do something, and in the meantime, we're having a town meeting tomorrow night around supper time."

～

The town meeting was more crowded than ever. Mollie stood at the front with Ellis beside her. Everyone in town seemed to be there, and the mood was tense.

Tulli and Celie took seats near the rear, close to the exit. Tulli rubbed his amulet before sitting down.

Mollie banged the gavel to get everyone's attention. "I'm askin' everyone to stay clear of the crime scene. The FBI should be coming down to examine the evidence we gathered, but they'll likely want to check the scene again when they get here, so let's keep it clean."

A man rose from a seat near the back of the room. It was Chester, a long-time resident. "I heard you found tracks."

Ellis and Mollie exchanged glances, then she sighed. "We did, Chester. Unusually large ones. Possibly animal, possibly human."

Whispers swept through the crowd, then the blacksmith stood.

"Ain't no sense dancin' around the issue, Sheriff. You know what did this, and keepin' it quiet ain't gonna do no good."

"We don't know anything for certain."

Little Hawk didn't bother standing, just shouted out from his seat near the front. "It's a werewolf. Same as the attacks in '79 and '55."

"Little Hawk, with all due respect."

"Don't need respect. This happens every thirty to forty years. Ask anyone who's been here long enough." He wagged a finger at Mollie. "And you should know better than most, Mollie. It was your people that died."

The crowd erupted in worried chatter.

Chester stood up and shouted. "We need to arm ourselves with silver bullets."

Mollie shouted. "Everyone calm the hell down."

The crowd quieted, but murmurs still rolled around.

Ellis stood beside Mollie. "We *will* find whoever, or whatever, did this to Henry — whether it was man or beast. In the meantime, everyone take precautions. Don't go out alone. Especially at night."

"Especially not during a full moon," someone shouted.

"All right, that's going to do it for tonight, folks. Just remember, we'll have deputies patrolling 24/7, so if you see any unusual activity, report it immediately."

As the meeting broke up, people clustered in worried groups, and the word "werewolf" was on everyone's lips.

Little Hawk approached Mollie as he was leaving.

"You found wolf hair at the scene?"

Mollie shuffled from one foot to another. When she spoke, it was in a low voice. "We found a few hairs, yes."

"You need to look at every mature male in town, especially the ones over eighteen and younger than forty. The werewolf will have a mark on the back of its neck. That's who we want."

"We can't do that, Little Hawk. Not without reasonable cause. "

"Then do anybody new in town." He pointed to Tulli, walking toward them. "We need to start with the newcomer. The killing started right after he got here."

Tulli was afraid but stood up and faced Little Hawk. "I'll show my neck, Little Hawk, if you pull down your pants and show your ass."

Mollie stepped between them to keep them separated. "That'll be enough talk of pulling down shirts or pants. Nobody will be showing their neck or anything else. Now let's get busy. We've got a killer to find."

Chapter Nine

THE CABIN

Three weeks went by and I hadn't been pestered by the sheriff or even Little Hawk. I walked down Main Street, feeling good about myself, when suddenly, someone tapped on my arm. I turned around to see Celie.

"You going to the game?" She seemed perky, as usual.

"Not tonight. Probably next week."

As I walked away, I kept looking back, and saw Celie watching me. She looked upset.

Celie muttered to herself. "Friday night and he's busy again." Determined to discover his real motive, she took off following him through

the woods. *I'll find out what's more important than going to a game —
with me.*

She made sure to keep her distance, but stayed close enough to see
where he went. After turning down a few trails, the woods opened to a
clearing with a cabin set near the back.

I went inside, tossed my backpack on a worn sofa, and boiled water
for tea. I packed the few clothes I had into my backpack, then put my
belongings into another. Afterward, I went through the door leading to
the cellar.

A small cell sat in the corner, iron bars on all sides, and a mattress
sat on the floor. A sink and a toilet were fixed on the back wall.

A pail of water sat near the front. Next to it was a bucket, scrubbed
clean and filled with fruits and vegetables. Iron shackles hung from the
ceiling.

I checked all the items, tugging on the shackles and inspecting the
food and water.

The water for tea steamed, causing the teapot to whistle and i
climbed the stairs and poured tea.

Celie watched from a distance, but didn't see anything, so she crept closer. When she was almost there, she kicked off her shoes and stepped lightly onto the porch.

She peered through the window, but didn't see Tulli.

The door to a bedroom was open but the room was empty. A clanging noise was heard coming from the basement.

She listened closely.

A low guttural growl echoed through the cabin. Celie moved to the steps and went one step lower to get a better look, and froze. Tulli's change began slowly, his skin rippling, veins darkening.

Celie ran from the cabin, screaming.

When Celie got home, she went to her bedroom, locked the door and windows, and crawled under the covers.

The floorboards creaked, and she jumped out of bed and sat against the door. *It can't be him, God. It <u>can't</u> be.*

Celie sat against the door, still dressed.

She looked at her phone: 5:47 AM. She stood, unlocked the door, and slipped out quietly.

Rita yelled to her as she left the house. "Young lady, get back here. Where do you think you're going?"

Rita raced to the door and stepped outside just as Celie reached her car.

She opened the car door and shouted back. "Wherever the hell I want to."

She climbed into the car and sped off, the tires squealing as she turned onto the main road. She turned the radio on, cranked the volume up louder, and drove toward Tulli's cabin.

With the coming of dawn, I reverted to human form. I collapsed, naked and exhausted on the floor, then I looked up and saw Celie sitting on the steps, her arms wrapped around herself.

I quickly dressed, then reached through the bars and opened the cell door.

Celie ran from the cabin and headed toward town.

I followed her in my truck, catching up halfway to town.

Celie wrapped her arms around herself, trembling.

I grabbed her by the shoulders and looked into her eyes. "Celie, will you listen. Please?"

She stared for a moment, obviously scared, then nodded.

"I've had a curse in my family for hundreds of years. Every month, I become a werewolf. But every month, I lock myself in that cell you saw so I don't hurt anyone. "

I could see she didn't buy my story, so I tried again. "What happened to Henry couldn't have been me. He wasn't killed on a full moon."

She calmed down a little. "It looked like a full moon."

I nodded. "But it wasn't. Full moons only happen when the moon is exactly opposite the sun. I can show you on my charts if that will convince you. Please, let me show you".

"I don't know. I ..."

"Please?"

I reached out my hand. Celie pulled back, but then reluctantly got in the truck while casting suspicious glances.

Once inside the cabin, I went to the bedroom and returned with a lunar chart. I pointed to the date Henry was killed. "As you can see, the moon wasn't full until the next night. I keep track of this closely."

Celie considered what I said, and as she looked around the room, she saw my bags were packed.

"Why are your bags packed?"

"I have to leave. Everyone is suspicious, especially after what Little Hawk said."

Celie turned her head side to side. "I need answers. How did this happen? What is it?"

"Let me pour you tea first." While I poured tea, I felt I needed to explain more.

"Ages ago, one of my ancestors was infused with wolf blood. That made her descendants werewolves. In every other generation, the first-born male is born with the mark of the wolf, a birthmark on the neck."

I pulled down the collar of my shirt and leaned over.

"This mark, the full moon. At birth it shows as a crescent moon, but as the person grows, so does the mark. When it turns to a full moon, the person is fully cursed and will change to a werewolf on every full moon after that."

"So this has been going on since you got here? Since ..."

Celie jumped up and headed for the door. "Oh, my God! Henry."

I grabbed her arm and pulled her back, staring.

"I already showed you the chart; it wasn't me that killed Henry. Besides, I would never do that. It's why I lock myself in the cell every month, and why I didn't go to the dance with you."

"That's the reason?"

I nodded. "The only reason."

"How did you get out of the cell?"

"I place the keys on a small table outside the cell. When my body changes, it grows, so I built the cell with the bars close together. It prevents me from reaching through the bars. But when I change back, I can reach them."

Celie reached, and reluctantly grabbed my hand.

I collapsed into her arms. "I'm so damn tired of running. I just want to find somewhere to stay and make a home. I'd give anything for that. Anything."

A tear ran down my cheek, which I wiped away. Celie took my hand, squeezed, and stared into my eyes.

"I'll help you, but you have to help me find out who, or what, did this? Henry was my cousin."

I stared into the distance, lips pressed together softly. My eyes slightly narrowed. "I don't know who did it, but I *will* find out."

"Are you going to stay?"

"I can't. The town is after blood — my blood. But I'll help you first."

"We'll talk about you staying later."

"Fine, but I don't know what I can do."

Frustrated, Celie raised her voice. "You have to be able to do something. Don't you have some kind of superpower ... anything?"

"Maybe. Maybe I can find something they missed."

He held her by the shoulders and pulled her to him. "All right, but when we're done, I've got to go. The people will never accept me now."

"I understand."

"I guess we'll become detectives then, but we need to do it while my senses are still heightened. "

Take a seat while I fix more tea.

Chapter Ten

LET'S BE DETECTIVES

We stepped carefully through the woods, careful not to make noise in case anyone was nearby. As we neared the scene where Henry was killed, we saw it was surrounded by a bright light and yellow crime-scene tape. There were warning signs taped on nearby trees, advising *no one* to disturb the scene.

I checked the surrounding area, then moved closer and lifted the tape to go inside the perimeter. I got on my knees and leaned close to the ground, sniffing furiously.

"What are you doing?"

"Seeing if I can detect any unusual smells. My senses aren't *fully* heightened, but for a few days before, and after, a full moon, they remain stronger than normal."

I continued moving slowly but was careful not to disturb the evidence. "I smell something unusual, Celie, and very distinct, but I can't pinpoint it."

Suddenly, Celie shouted. "Somebody's coming."

Headlights grew brighter as a car came up the trail.

I rushed outside the taped area and grabbed Celie's hand, then we ran deep into the woods, not stopping until we reached the cabin.

Once inside, Celie paced the floor, out of breath. "That was close."

I nodded. "And I don't like them getting that close. We need to be more careful. Besides that, my senses are growing weak. We may have to figure out something else."

"You mean we can't go back to the scene?"

I looked at Celie and shook my head. "It wouldn't do any good. Now I can't smell any better than you can."

Celie raised her eyebrows. "What did you smell back there?"

"I don't know. I didn't recognize it. But if I smell it again, I'll know it."

"If it was out there, then it was likely from someone in town. We can go through all the stores and see if you recognize it."

"Good idea, but we'll have to wait till it's closer to a full moon."

Celie pulled me onto the sofa beside her. "In the meantime, let's get to know each other better."

I leaned in close and kissed her. "There's nothing I'd like better."

"You should come to my house for dinner. How about Friday?"

I hesitated. "I don't know ... I don't think your mom likes me."

"Don't worry about her. She can be a pain in the ass, but she'll get over it. C'mon. You'll have fun."

Tulli drove to Celie's house and entered when she opened the door.

Rita came out of the kitchen wearing an apron and a pair of jeans. "Tulli, nice to see you again."

"You too, Ms. Mattson. And thank you for inviting me. I could use a home-cooked meal. I've been living on canned foods."

"How long have you been alone?"

"A long time, ma'am. My dad died years ago, and my mother went back to Alaska, so I've been on my own for a while."

"Celie tells me you rented the Billings house out in the woods."

"Yes, ma'am. It's working out great for me. It's close to work and not far from town."

"What kind of work do you do?"

"I work at the lumber mill as a millwright."

"How nice. Do you plan to continue in that job?"

Tulli seemed confused. "As long as I can; it's a good job."

"I'm sure with a better education you could get a better position."

"I'm happy with my position, ma'am. Like I said, it's a good job, and it pays well."

"I guess if you're single it's not bad, but —"

"Mom, in most marriages nowadays, both people work. And his pay is better than most."

Tulli wiped his mouth with his napkin, then stood. "May I use the restroom, please?"

Celie pointed behind him. "It's down that long hallway. Last door on the right."

After Tulli left, Celie gritted her teeth and leaned close to her mother. Her voice was lowered, but intense. "What's with the third degree, Mom? Just leave him the hell alone. "

"You *have* been mean, Mom," Clark said.

Linda set her drink down hard on the table. "I *like* Tulli. He's nice."

Rita huffed and sat erect. "I see I've been outvoted."

Tulli returned from the restroom, ate dessert, then said goodbye to everyone. He shook hands with Rita. "I think I better be going, Ms. Mattson. I need to get up early. But thanks for dinner. "

Celie got up and followed him." I'm going too."

"Don't forget your keys, dear."

"I'm fine. I'll get a ride with Tulli in the morning."

Rita gasped. "In the morning? You can't spend the night. What if someone finds out? What about your reputation? "

Celie turned to her, expression defiant. "My reputation now is that I'm a stuck-up bitch. Maybe I can change that."

Celie stormed out the door, slamming it as she left.

Tulli plopped down on the sofa and turned on the TV. Celie kicked off her shoes and lay on the sofa, putting her feet on Tulli's lap. "I could use a foot massage."

"And, Tulli, I'm sorry about my mother's behavior. Sometimes I think she doesn't want me to be happy or have a normal life."

Tulli tried to be consoling. "Be patient with her. She's just worried about you."

Tulli massaged her feet, then rubbed farther up her legs. She moaned with pleasure, then got up and sat on the floor between his legs. She removed her sweatshirt and leaned back. "Now you can work the kinks out of my shoulders."

Tulli rubbed cream on his hands then massaged her back and shoulders. Her moans grew louder. "Oh, God, Tulli that's perfect."

He moved lower on her arms, then moved toward her front and rubbed her breasts. "I was wondering when you'd get around to that."

Celie leaned her head back and looked at him. "Maybe we should take this to the bedroom."

Mollie walked down Main Street, her eyes scanning everything. Little Hawk sat in his rocker on the porch in front of the Native American store.

Aa Mollie walked by, Little Hawk called out to her. "Sheriff, you looked at the newcomer's neck yet?"

Mollie gave him a cross-eyed look. "That's not gonna happen, Little Hawk. I've got no reason."

Little Hawk puffed on his pipe and continued rocking. "You'll find a way."

Mollie patrolled Main Street and eventually came across Tulli.

"What are you doing in town so early? I thought you didn't get off work until five."

Tulli looked at Mollie and frowned. "I was let go."

"Let go? I thought Jasper was still hiring?"

"He is, but Little Hawk must have whispered in his ear. He fired me."

Chapter Eleven

MORE INVESTIGATION

Mollie went behind her office to what she called "The Dead Room." It was a small warehouse that had been converted to a lab for crime scene analysis, and even autopsies when the medical examiner made her way to Valley's End.

Mollie entered and walked back to where Jones — her intelligent, nerdy technician — peered through a microscope, analyzing samples collected from the crime scene.

Mollie walked up and tapped Jones on the shoulder. "Just got a call from the FBI in Coeur d'Alene. They said they can't send anyone for weeks, and we also struck out at the offices in Boise and Pocatello."

"I guess it's just you and me, Sheriff."

"Guess so, Jones, so tell me where we are."

"Here's what I've got so far: bite marks, saliva, and skin cells — pure human. All blood samples belong to the victim. All human DNA, no anomalies."

"No animal DNA?"

"That's the strange part. On the victim's clothing and under his fingernails, we found fur. I tested it twice, and this fur is pure wolf. Not dog — wolf."

Mollie looked puzzled. "Wolf fur ... but no wolf saliva?"

Jones nodded. "Exactly, and the claw marks are consistent with an animal attack. You can see the depth and pattern but none of the usual biological evidence from a wolf bite. Just human saliva and skin cells."

"So the attacker is human ... but somehow left wolf fur?"

"Could be a disguise, but if it is, it's made from real wolf fur — the kind you can't buy at a costume store."

Mollie stepped closer to Jones. "Or maybe someone wants us to think it's not human." Mollie paced, giving thought to what she said. "There's another possibility — it could be both human and wolf."

Jones scrunched up his eyebrows. "Explain?"

Mollie tapped Jones on the chest with her finger. "You'll think I'm crazy, but have you considered it might really be a werewolf?" She paused to give Jones time to consider what she said. "The locals think so. Mind you, I don't think that, but some of the locals do."

Jones held back his laughter. "That's a bit radical, Sherif."

Mollie nodded. "Keep doing your analysis. See if anything new comes up."

Jones rubbed his hands together. "How about we take a break and look at this later?"

After a short lunch break, Mollie and Jones went to the lab inside the sheriff's station. Jones pulled out his evidence and put it under a microscope. "Take a look, Mollie. Thick patches of wolf fur."

Mollie leaned over the microscope and looked, then she pulled her head back, focused her eyes, and looked again. "I've looked at this twice. The saliva's human and the fur is wolf."

Jones looked at her with his eyebrows raised.

Mollie nodded. "I know. Someone is going to a lot of trouble to make us believe it's a werewolf."

Jones's face turned somber. "Or like you said — it really is."

Mollie and Jones exchanged a suspicious glance.

"Let me take a look at that again," Jones said.

Mollie watched as Jones peered into the microscope. He then reviewed the DNA analysis on the computer screen, clearly puzzled.

"The depth, spacing, and angle of the claw wounds are consistent with an animal attack."

"And the wolf fur embedded under the fingernails?" Mollie asked.

"I ran the fur through morphometric analysis. It's genuine wolf fur — not a synthetics blend, not a dog — real wolf. And this sample is a perfect match with all genetic markers to wild Canis lupus."

Jones printed out the results, then showed the analysis to Mollie. "Could be a human attacker who wore a wolf pelt, and maybe used claws on gloves to simulate the attack."

"That's the logical explanation," Mollie said.

Jones tapped his fingers on the table. "Or it's something else — some sort of hybrid biology. Either way, whoever did this wanted us to be confused."

"So, no clear answers. Just a scene set to mislead us." Mollie handed the analysis back to Jones. "If it's a man in a costume, he's putting on a show that's biologically convincing, but the one theory we haven't explored is the one everybody's worried about — what if it is a werewolf?"

Jones shook his head. "I don't know, Mollie. Who knows what the hell is in those woods. People still swear Bigfoot's roaming those woods somewhere."

"Don't laugh," Mollie said. "If — and I know that's a big if — it's a werewolf, wouldn't it make sense that the saliva might be human and the fur wolf."

Jones looked at Mollie with fear in his eyes.

"A werewolf *is* supposed to be half human and half wolf."

Jones stared at Mollie in silence.

Papers covered Mollie's desk, along with folders filled with evidence files. She leafed through the forensics reports, occasionally making notes of interesting items. The sound of a phone ringing startled her. "Sheriff Newsom."

A deep voice with a thick accent spoke to her. "This is Inspector Petrov from Dobrich. I review files you sent.

"And?"

"Same as two cases here. Same bites, human saliva, and wolf fur."

Mollie wrote notes as he spoke. "Did you ever catch who did it?"

Petrov laughed. "You never catch a werewolf. You kill it, or it is gone."

Petrov paused. "What did the murders in my country, the same as what did yours. And it was no man."

"You *really* think that, Inspector?"

"I *know* that."

Mollie stopped writing and closed the file. "Okay, thanks, Inspector."

Chapter Twelve

TAKEN

Three Weeks Later

Linda and Amy waited outside the school for their ride home. The afternoon sun cast long shadows across the playground, and it was warm enough to unzip their coats.

Linda looked up and down the street. "My mom's late again."

Amy stood next to Linda but didn't respond. She was engrossed in a dog-eared book with a picture of a silver wolf on the cover. Her fingers traced the illustration as she flipped through pages filled with mysterious creatures.

Linda glanced at the book Amy held. "What are you reading?"

Amy tilted the book toward Linda — *Creatures of the Night*.

It had notes and colorful bookmarks sticking out from dozens of pages.

Amy then flipped a few pages and showed the book to Linda. "Look at this part about the transformation."

Linda rolled her eyes. "Oh, my God, Amy. That's just made-up stuff, and you know it."

Amy shut the book, clutching it protectively to her chest. "It's almost a full moon. Tonight it probably will be, so if we're going home, we better get walking."

Linda stepped into the street and looked up and down. "I don't see Mom yet."

"I'm not waiting any longer." Amy started off down the road, heading toward the woods.

Linda hesitated and looked up the road, then raced after Amy. "Wait! Where are you going?"

Amy turned her head. "I'm going home before it gets dark."

Linda grudgingly followed her, taking the lumber trail as a shortcut. "This is where your brother ..."

Amy reached out and grabbed Linda's hand. "Don't worry. I'm with you."

Linda looked side to side as she walked, and she continually looked up at the gray clouds, shivering when she did.

"We need to walk faster, Amy."

"I'm going as fast as I can."

A noise from the woods made them to break into a run. Twigs snapped and leaves rustled, causing them to go faster, but whatever was making the noise kept up with them.

As Amy navigated a sharp turn in the trail, something with a large paw and coarse fur grabbed her and yanked her into the woods.

Linda screamed, stopping momentarily, but then she increased her pace. As she rounded a bend, she, too, was taken.

Ellis paced frantically, a phone pressed to his ear.

Sheila sat on the couch, clutching one of Amy's sweaters, tears streaming down her face. She got up, pacing and wringing her hands and all the while, biting her lip.

Josh stood by the window and stared into the darkness.

Ellis smacked his hand against the wall. "It's been six hours, Sheila. Six goddamn hours, and she's only eight years old."

Sheila broke down, sobbing. "My baby ... my little girl."

Ellis turned to Sheila, tears rolling down his face. "Why the hell didn't you pick her up. Why?"

"Rita said she would pick them up."

Josh pulled his knees up to his chin. Tears ran steadily down his cheek. "It was that same thing that killed Henry, wasn't it?"

Ellis put his hand on Josh's shoulder. "We don't know that."

"What else could it be? First Henry, now Amy."

Sheila wailed. "Oh, God. Not my baby."

Ellis pulled her to him and held her tight. "Don't worry. The whole town is looking for her."

"But what if it's too late? What if it got her?"

Ellis kisses her cheek. "We'll find her. I swear."

Josh answers the doorbell to find Celie standing on the porch, her eyes red and swollen.

"I was in town when I heard. Any news?"

Josh shook his head and stepped aside. Celie entered and sat beside Donna, holding her hand. "I can't believe both girls are missing. What's happening to our town?"

Donna lowered her head and spoke in whispers. "First Henry. Now, Amy and Linda. This is crazy."

Josh slammed his fist against the wall.

Celie went over and hugged Josh, then sat and talked with Donna. After while, Ellis offered her a ride home.

When Celie got home, her mom was on the phone talking to neighbors and telling them of Amy and Linda. "Yes, both Amy Litkin and Linda. If you see <u>anything</u>, call the sheriff immediately."

Rita nodded as someone on the other end talked. "I know, it's terrifying." She hung up and plopped into a chair, wiping tears from her eyes, and mumbling.

Celie and Clark sat at the table, frightened. The mood was somber.

Rita leaned back in the chair, then she hunched over and buried her face in her hands and cried. "Not Amy. Not by baby!"

Celie wiped away tears. "Mom, what's happening? What are we gonna do?"

Rita blew her nose, and wiped her eyes with the tissue. Her voice broke when she spoke. "I don't know, honey. I just don't know."

Clark moved closer. "Do you think it's a werewolf? Like people are saying?"

"I can't think now. Just pray the girls are safe."

"Everyone at school is saying it's a werewolf," Clark said.

Celie smacked the back of his head. "That's ridiculous."

Chapter Thirteen

IS IT A WEREWOLF?

I walked in as Mollie nursed her second cup of coffee and finished her pie. She picked up her coffee and sat next to me. "Tulli, I'd like you to come to the office tomorrow."

I stared at Mollie. "If this is about Henry, I had nothing to do with it."

Mollie shook her head. "I'd still like you to drop by."

The next day, I walked in and took a seat. I had a few folders in my arm, and set them on the edge of the desk. "You didn't tell me about the girls last night."

"I assumed Celie would have told you."

I picked up one of the folders and opened it. It was full of charts showing the days of the month with the moon phases overlapping each day. I pointed to the date when Henry was killed. "As you can see, the moon wasn't full that night. It *almost* was, but not quite."

I flipped the page to the night the girls disappeared. "And if you look at the night the girls disappeared — again, no full moon."

Mollie's interest perked up. "And this is verifiable?"

"Absolutely. I studied astronomy before I dropped out of college, but since I left it's become a hobby. Check with any expert and they'll tell you."

"Why'd you drop out?"

"My father died during my second year and my mother needed help,"

"Oh my God. I'm so sorry, Tulli."

"Thanks, Sheriff."

Mollie walked around the desk to stand next to me. "Let me get a closer look at those."

When she squeezed past me, she stumbled and grabbed my shirt, stretching it down as she fell forward. I felt positive she looked up when she fell, getting a full view of the back of my neck.

I quickly pulled the shirt up, then spun around to face Mollie. My voice was deep and threatening. "Get a good enough look, Sheriff?"

Mollie didn't say anything, but I noticed she kept her hand close to her gun. "If you have something to ask, ask it," I said.

"Did you have anything to do with Henry's death?"

I balled my fists and put my knuckles on her desk. "I've never had anything to do with anyone's death. If you're done, I'm leaving."

I gathered my files and went back to the cabin.

My bed was cluttered with several open bags and piles of clothes, and the few belongings I had.

Celie walked in, taking in the scene at once. "What's going on? Why are you packing?"

I turned sharply. "She knows, Celie. The sheriff *knows*."

"So you're just leaving?"

"You're damn right I'm leaving. She saw the mark on my neck."

Celie sat on the bed and cried. "You promised."

I continued packing, but more slowly. I watched her out of the corner of my eye, then sighed, and pulled her to me. I held her tightly. "All right. All right, I'll help, but then I have to go."

Celie looked up at me. "You heard about the girls?"

I nodded.

"I'm so sorry about Linda. But don't worry, we'll figure something out. My senses are almost back now."

Los Angeles

Linda and Amy, terrified but unharmed, huddled in the corner of a dark, windowless room, shivering on the cold floor.

Metal shelving units lined two walls, and a single bare bulb hung from the ceiling. A thin mattress lay in the corner with two blankets haphazardly thrown over it.

Linda's eyes were red from crying but her face was set in determination. Amy paced, biting her nails.

At the sound of heavy footsteps approaching, Amy froze and ran to Linda, who wrapped her arm around the taller girl.

"Remember, Amy, don't cry, and don't beg."

Amy nodded, but her lower lip trembled as the door creaked open.

Marco entered, carrying a tray with two sandwiches and two bottles of water. He set the tray on the floor and kicked it toward them. "Dinner."

Linda stared at him, refusing to move. Amy looked at the food, almost drooling.

Marco sneered at them. "Eat. Don't eat. Not my problem."

He turned to leave when Linda spoke. "When are we going home?"

Marco paused, then looked back at them with an amused expression. "You don't get it, do you? I been here twenty years."

"My dad will find us," Linda said.

Marco laughed, a sound without humor. "This isn't some TV show where the hero saves the day."

"*Please*, mister?" Amy begged him.

Marco's face softened slightly, then hardened again. "Just eat your food and be quiet. The boss will be back tomorrow."

Linda stood up straighter. "Is your boss the man who took us?"

Marco's eyes widened slightly before he caught himself. "You'd be wise not to mention him."

He slammed the door shut, and the lock clicked loudly.

Amy crawled to the tray, grabbed a sandwich, and stuffed her mouth. She took several swigs of water while she was still chewing.

Linda watched her, then reluctantly, joined in. "We need to keep our strength up."

Amy nodded, then her eyes filled with tears again.

~

Valleys End

The gathering crowd grew as Ellis stood on the steps of the town hall, pacing near the podium. Posters with Linda and Amy's photos hung behind him.

Mollie stepped on the platform beside him. "I know we've done this before, but we're once again organizing search parties. Sign-up sheets are at the tables."

One member near the back shouted out. "What about the animal that killed your boy?"

Another joined in. "Is it the same one that took the girls?"

Lewis, who owned several tracking dogs, added his voice. "An animal can't snatch two girls and haul them away without leaving tracks of some kind."

He leaned down and patted the heads of his dogs. "Either way, my dogs will find 'em. They can find anything."

"We don't know what happened yet," Ellis said.

As the murmurs grew louder. Mollie stepped forward and shouted.

"We're focusing on finding Linda and Amy, not chasing rumors or myths."

Little Hawk remained seated, but he spoke loudly. The crowd went quiet, recognizing his role in the community. "The beast has tasted blood and hungers for more."

Mollie pushed Ellis slightly to the side and took the mic. "We'll check all possibilities, Little Hawk. But right now, those girls need us to stay focused. Search parties begin in fifteen minutes."

Lewis stepped up to Ellis. "Get me some clothes worn by the girls — both of 'em. My dogs will make short work of this hunt."

Search parties moved to the bottom part of Lumber Trail. Lewis took the clothes from Ellis and Rita and let the dogs — Sally and Jess — picked up the scent. Then he unleashed them.

Sally ran up the trail, stopping by a sharp turn. Her nose dipped low to the ground. Whiskers twitched as she inhaled deeply. Her ears pricked forward, and she reared her head back and emitted a howl that echoed through the woods.

Jess was right behind her, but ran past Sally until she came to a slight bend in the trail. She lifted her tail, and every muscle tensed. She stopped and sniffed more, then howled loudly, announcing her find.

Lewis proudly led the search party forward. "Told ya' they'd find 'em."

One of the search volunteers stepped toward Ellis. "You think the girls are still alive?"

Ellis grabbed his chest, stopped by a sharp pain. "I have to think that; otherwise ..."

"But if it's that same thing that killed your boy ...?"

Ellis turned, eyes glaring, and raised his voice. "We don't know what it is."

The volunteer lowered his voice. "Sorry, Ellis."

They continued to follow the dogs as they led them deeper into the woods. The dogs stopped at a large clearing with a small stream forming into a pond in the middle.

Lewis knelt down next to the dogs. "What's up, girls? Go find 'em."

The dogs walked around sniffing, but they stopped at the pond. Lewis walked back to Mollie and Ellis. "Looks like they lost the scent. Whatever they were tracking must have gone into the water."

One of the volunteers yelled from the edge of the woods. "I've got a ribbon. A small red one."

Rita ran forward and grabbed the ribbon, examining it. "This is Linda's."

Tears flowed down her face again. "Oh my God! It's my baby's."

Another volunteer shouted from about fifty feet away. "Look. Tracks."

Ellis examines the ground and saw impressions in the soil. "Too big for a child."

"Too big for a man, too," Lewis said.

Lewis led his dogs over. They sniffed the print, then backed away, whimpering. Ellis's face darkened. "We need the FBI to examine this. They have the expertise."

Mollie leaned close to Ellis and whispered. "The FBI won't be here for weeks, if then."

A young man ran forward holding a piece of cloth. He seemed excited. "Just found this. It looked like it might be part of a shirt."

Mollie squeezed her lips together and balled her fist. Her face turned grim. "Set it down, now! Put the damn cloth down."

Mollie looked at the group in front of her. "I'll only say this once. Do not. I repeat <u>do not</u> touch anything. If you see something that might belong to one of the girls, notify me. But <u>do not</u> — under any circumstances — disturb the scene."

Mollie turned to the one who found the cloth. "Now show me where you found this."

Chapter Fourteen

TRAPPED

Los Angeles

A dim, flickering bulb cast uneven shadows on the cracked concrete walls of a cramped room. The air was stale and thick with the smell of smoke.

Linda and Amy sat on a cold floor, trembling. Linda clutched a torn piece of sheet and rubbed it against her face.

Amy's eyes darted toward the locked door, her breathing quiet.

Linda whispered to Amy. "Do you think they'll come back?"

Amy swallowed hard, and her eyes went wide. "They said they'd bring us food."

Linda sobbed, then broke into tears. "I'd rather starve than have him come back here."

Amy hugged her tightly and patted her back. "I know, but I'm so hungry my stomach hurts. And I'm thirsty."

A faint murmur echoed from the hallway outside — footsteps pacing. Both girls froze and Linda pulled Amy's sleeve gently. "Stay close, okay?"

A shadow passed under the crack of the door. Neither girl looked up, but they squeezed their hands together.

The door rattled, the sound lingering. Then they heard another sound — a key being inserted into the door. When the door opened, Marco entered with a small tray of food.

"Is everyone going to eat tonight?"

Both girls remained quiet as Marco set the tray on the floor and slid it to them. "You need to eat. You'll have visitors tonight. And they'll expect you to be clean, so you need to bathe too."

Amy blinked back tears and Linda rubbed the torn piece of sheet against her cheek harder. They stared at each other while far away, city lights flickered through a barred window.

"What are we gonna do?" Linda asked.

"I just wish my dad was here," Amy said.

～

Valleys End

Mollie pinned new evidence photos to the board, and Jones walked over to study them.

Jones looked them over, then looked again. "Looks like something dragged them."

"But dragged them where? We've searched every cave and every abandoned building for miles."

Jones gave it thought. "Maybe they're not in town anymore."

Mollie digested what Jones said. "You think someone took them?"

"It would explain the lack of remains."

"Yeah, that would explain the lack of remains, but everyone seems fixated on this werewolf theory."

"Now that you mention it, a person using a werewolf as a cover would be the perfect way to go. Everyone's looking for a monster in the woods while the real monster drives away with two young girls."

Mollie turned to the map on the wall, studying the roads leading out of town. "If they drove out of town, there's only one road they would have likely taken, and the state police have a camera this side of the Oregon line."

"Yes, they do," Jones said. "But going through that footage would take a lot of legwork."

"We've got a lot of volunteers, and I bet most of 'em would rather look through video footage than traipse through the woods."

Jones nodded. "Call the state troopers. I'll get with Ellis."

As Jones walked to his office, he glanced down at a newspaper on Mollie's desk: "Werewolf fear grips valley's end as search for missing girls continues."

He yells back to Mollie. "Whatever we do, we better hurry. I'm afraid this town's about to explode."

Celie and I strolled down Main Street, stopping to browse in each of the shops along the way. About halfway down, while shopping in a small general store, I grabbed Celie's arm.

"That smell is in here somewhere."

"Where?"

"I don't know yet, but I'll find it."

I picked up various items and appeared to be studying them. While looking at a stuffed fox, Celie walked by, and I grabbed her arm.

"This is it, Celie. It's the chemicals they use for taxidermy."

Recognition lit in Celie's eyes. "There's a taxidermy shop in town. Frank Mathers owns it with his son."

Mollie set up a roadblock and deputies checked vehicles entering and leaving town. Ellis stood watch, scrutinizing each driver.

Mollie approached, offering coffee. "The state police are checking traffic camera footage."

"You think they'll find anything?" Ellis asked. "The back roads don't have cameras. What if they left that way?"

"Then we keep searching," Mollie said.

Ellis looked out at the vast wilderness surrounding their small town. "They could be anywhere by now."

"We'll find them, Ellis."

The paper's editor, Carl Winters, worked on the next day's front page. The headline read: "Still no sign of missing girls."

A young reporter entered with a notepad as Carl prepared everything for print. "The town's going crazy with this werewolf theory."

Carl made a snide remark. "What else explains a killer that leaves no evidence, takes hostages, but makes no demands?"

"You believe it?" The reporter asked.

"I believe something took those girls. And whoever did it, doesn't want 'em found."

The reporter kept the conversation going. "My cousin at the morgue says the marks on Henry Litkin weren't like any animal attack he's seen." He took time to read the first part of the story. "I know Mollie's trying to keep a lid on this to stop panic, but I don't know if that will work with the people all riled up."

He gestured to a stack of papers on his desk. "See that stack of letters? Every one of 'em is about the werewolf."

The entire town gathered for a candlelight vigil. Photos of Linda and Amy were displayed on an improvised altar.

Ellis stood with his family and the Mattsons, both looking exhausted. Sheila leaned on Donna for support.

The minister stood on a makeshift stage and opened the Bible. "Let us pray for the safe return of Linda and Amy. May the Lord protect them from harm and guide them home."

Tulli stood at the back, watching. He scanned the crowd, his expression focused and determined.

Celie stood beside him. "Sense anything?"

"Not yet."

Celie looked worried. "You think someone here knows where they are?"

"I think someone here isn't as worried as they're pretending."

Tulli strolled through the crowd, and used his heightened senses to study each person.

Celie walked beside him and whispered. "Nothing yet?"

Tulli shook his head. "The town is focused on a monster. But sometimes the real monsters look just like everyone else."

As the vigil ended and people dispersed, Tulli watched intently, like a predator studying its prey. "I'm going to find whatever, or whoever, took them, Celie."

"How?"

"By embracing what I am. Even the parts I'm afraid of." His eyes briefly flashed yellow in the gathering darkness.

As the vigil ended, Mollie approached Tulli. "Seen anything unusual lately? In the woods maybe?"

Tulli shrugged. "I haven't seen anything specific. But if you need help searching, maybe I can assist."

Mollie looked Tulli over suspiciously. "I'll let you know," she said, then walked away and, as she left, Celie approached Tulli.

"What was that about?"

"She's suspicious," Tulli said.

"Of you?"

"Maybe. Let's go."

As they walked away, Mollie watched.

Mollie followed them to Tulli's cabin. She waited until they went inside, then she approached carefully. She looked through the front window and saw them go down the cellar steps.

Once they disappeared, Mollie entered the house and followed. Halfway down the steps, the cell came into view and Mollie halted.

Tulli heard a creaking sound and turned quickly to see Mollie pointing her gun at him, although she was backed up against the wall.

"You're ..."

Celie stepped between them, placing her hand on Tulli's chest, and holding him back.

"Sheriff, he's not the person you're looking for. He didn't hurt anyone."

Mollie's hands trembled and her eyes opened wide. She continued backing up the steps, and kept her weapon pointed at Tulli. "Celie, how can you say that? It's your sister, for God's sake."

"I was with him when the girls were taken. I was right here in this cabin with him the entire night."

Mollie stared at Celie, then looked at Tulli." You're really ...?"

Tulli shook his head. " Unfortunately, Sheriff. I have no idea what you're talking about.

"Maybe you should put your gun away, then we can go upstairs, and I'll fix us some tea."

Mollie nodded and put her gun in her holster, then Tulli followed her up the stairs.

Celie sat on Tulli's worn sofa while Mollie paced.

"What's your plan?" Celie asked Tulli.

"I think we should go."

"I'm going with you."

Tulli saw the determined look in Celie's eyes.

"Fine. But we go at dusk. And at the first sign of trouble, you run."

Mollie stared at the two of them, looking dumbfounded. "I'm right here. Where the hell do you think you're going? "

"Celie and I inspected Henry's crime scene. There were traces of taxidermy chemicals still on the leaves. Arsenic and more."

Mollie perked up. "We didn't find that."

"I was trained in chemistry. I noticed the very familiar scent of arsenic at the scene."

The mention of arsenic brought recognition to Mollie. "The Mathers?"

"We're going to find out."

"And I'd bet if you analyze your evidence again and look specifically for arsenic, you'll find it. That should give you enough for a warrant."

Mollie called Jones and told him to re-analyze the evidence and to specifically look for arsenic, then she turned to Tulli. "Wait for me to get the warrant."

"We don't have time, Sheriff, but I'll call if we find anything."

"While you're playing detective, remember there's a meeting tonight. It won't look good if you two aren't there."

Celie looked at Tulli, her eyebrows raised. "We going to the meeting?"

"We need to get supplies in town anyway. Might as well."

Mollie got in her car and headed toward town, looking in the rearview mirror as she left. Once she was far enough away from the cabin, she pulled out her recorder and spoke into it.

"I'm pretty damn sure Tulli is a suspect, probably the main suspect, but I'm not positive. Besides, I didn't have a warrant, so I couldn't do anything anyway."

She set the recorder down and continued the drive, but picked it back up again in a moment.

"I blamed not doing anything on the warrant, but the truth is, if Tulli's what I think he is, I don't know if I want to do anything. Not yet, anyway, and not by myself."

Celie wrapped her arms around Tulli and sobbed. "I'm worried, Tulli. There's no doubt she knows. What are we going to do? And what's she going to do?"

"I don't know, but we can't worry about it. We've got things to do."

Tulli and Celie went to town, and saw the gathering at the park. At that point, they decided they should attend the meeting.

The park was packed and tempers flared. Bushcat, in town for the meeting, riled people up. "It's a werewolf and everyone here knows it. There's no sense foolin' around. We got to find him while the moon's not full."

Little Hawk stood and raised his voice." If you want to put an end to this, we need to check the newcomer. Nothing happened until he got here."

Mollie sensed the crowd had reached mob mentality, and she noticed they surrounded Tulli and closed in on him. One of the townspeople yelled. "Get him. We'll stop the killing."

Three men grabbed Tulli and then two more joined in. They were hauling him toward the street when Mollie banged her gavel and shouted. When no one listened, she drew her firearm, and shot in the air. She had to shoot twice before they stopped.

"Tulli, get up here now."

When Tulli didn't respond fast enough, she shouted louder. "Now! Tulli, or I'll have them drag you up here."

Her actions and tone calmed down the crowd, but it did nothing to calm Tulli.

After another moment, he stood, and both he and Celie went to the stage, continually casting glances back and forth.

"Put your hands behind your back," Mollie said.

Mollie stepped behind Tulli and pulled his hands behind his back. She whispered as she put the cuffs on him. "You're gonna have to trust me. I need to get you out of here."

Mollie took him to the jail. She locked him up, then paced in front of the cell. "Tulli, I don't know what to do with you."

"From where I sit, you have nothing to hold me on."

"I saw that mark on your neck."

"A birthmark means nothing, Sheriff. I think you know that."

Celie walked up close to Mollie." Sheriff, you've known me a long time. I would never protect anyone who hurt my sister. With that in mind, I'm telling you, Tulli is innocent."

Mollie paced more, then she sighed and walked to the cell. "All right. I'll trust you, Tulli. But don't let me down."

She checked that no one was watching, then opened the cell and removed the cuffs. Then she set Tulli free.

Back at the cabin, Celie sat on the sofa in the living room, tapping her foot on the floor as she waited for Tulli. "I see your bags are still packed."

"But I haven't left."

"If we're going to the Mathers' place, we need to go now."

"It's dangerous."

"Everything about this is dangerous."

"Okay. Let's go."

"And, Celie. I can't tell you what your support means to me. I've never had anyone to talk to except my father ... and now you. And my father's been dead for a long time."

"You never told me what happened with your mother?"

"She abandoned me. She didn't even say goodbye."

Celie grabbed him and pulled him close, then kissed him." Oh, God, Tulli. I'm so sorry, but that's all the more reason to stay."

Chapter Fifteen

A NEW PLAN

Celie sat on the worn sofa while I paced. "What's your plan?"

"The full moon is one week away, but my senses are already heightened. I want to go to the Mathers' place."

"That's suicide." Celie bit her fingernails. "But I'm coming with you. Linda is my sister."

I looked at her, then nodded reluctantly. "Fine. But we go at dusk. And at the first sign of trouble, you run."

Los Angeles

Linda and Amy sat huddled together in a bare room, with nothing but a thin mattress and a bucket in the corner. A dim bulb provided minimal light.

Marco entered carrying trays of food. He looked down at the empty food bowls and smiled. "I see hunger got the best of you. Don't worry. You'll even want to bathe before long."

"My dad has money," Linda said. "If you let us go, he'll pay you."

Marco laughed sarcastically. "My boss has more."

He set the trays down, picked up the empty ones, and turned to leave, locking the door behind him.

Valleys End

The phone rang as Mollie pored over reports stacked high on her desk. "Newsom."

"Mollie, this is Dan with the state police. We picked out a live one. Plate number: A7425. Chrysler van, 2019. Registered to Frank Mathers. Address ..."

Mollie typed the information into her computer. "Got it. Thanks."

Mollie got on the phone and called Jones. "Barney just called. He's got Frank Mathers' van leaving on the same night the girls went missing."

"We can't question a man for driving down a public road, Mollie."

"I know. But Mathers owns a taxidermy shop, and that would give him access to wolf fur. <u>Real</u> fur. The kind of fur you found at the crime scene."

Frank Mathers and his son Jake packed supplies into duffel bags. A wolf costume with real fur hung on a hook nearby, alongside metal claws that could be attached to gloves.

"We need to move fast. Shipment's expected tomorrow," Jake said.

"Grab the sedatives."

"You think they suspect anything?" Jake asked.

"They're all chasing werewolf stories, and we'll be long gone before they figure it out. Once we get rid of these two girls, and the girls we delivered from Montana, we can retire."

A phone on the workbench rang, and Jake answered. "Yeah?"

"No, Victor, we're on schedule. We can be there in two days, and don't worry, it's clean. No one knows." Jake hung up and looked at his father. "Victor says the buyers are eager. The'll fetch top price."

"Perfect," Frank said. "Soon, we can leave this godforsaken town for good."

Celie sat on a sofa in the living room, waiting for Tulli. When he came in, she stared with a determined look. "I see your bags are still packed."

I nodded. "But I haven't left."

"I see that," Celie said. "But are we going to check out the Mathers' place?"

"It's dangerous."

"Everything about this is dangerous," Celie said. "But Linda and Amy are running out of time. I can feel it."

"Okay. We'll do it tomorrow." I pulled her to me and hugged her. "And, Celie. I can't tell you what your support means to me. I've never had anyone to talk to except my father ... and now you."

Celie grabbed him and pulled him close, then kissed him.

Chapter Sixteen

THE TAXIDERMY SHOP

Frank worked on a deer head, carefully placing glass eyes in the sockets. The bell over the door rang as I entered, looking casual but alert. I ducked under the protruding jaw of a bull moose but almost bumped into the extended teeth of a large mountain lion, both appeared real.

Frank Mathers greeted me with a friendly smile. "Can I help you, son?"

"Just looking. Never been in a place like this before."

Frank nodded, returning to his work. I wandered the shop, examining the mounted animals and pelts. I paid particular attention to the wolves. "These wolves are amazing. So lifelike."

I wonder if the fur matches the crime scenes?

Frank beamed with pride. "That's the art of it. Making them seem alive again."

"You must know a lot about wolves," I said. "I'm doing a report for school, and ..."

"I know enough to stuff 'em. Nothing more." Frank stopped and stared. "You're not from around here, are you?"

I shook my head.

"Thought so," Frank said. "If you were, you'd know how people in these parts feel about wolves — don't like 'em."

"Mind if I ask you some questions?"

Frank seemed impatient. "Depends on the questions."

"How do you make the fur look so real?"

Frank cast a wary glance at me.

"Trade secret."

I moved toward a door marked *employees only.* "What's back there?"

"It's not for customers."

Something in Frank's tone made me pause. I nodded and backed away. "Sorry. Just curious."

Frank gave me a threatening look. "Curiosity's natural. Prying's not."

"Thanks for your time" I said, and left.

I walked away and met up with Celie about a block away. "He's hiding something. I could smell his fear when I got near the back room."

That seemed to get her interest. "Fear of what?" Celie asked.

"Of being discovered," I said. "We're going in tonight."

Celie grabbed hold of my arm. "Maybe we should tell the police what you saw and leave it to them."

I grinned. "They can't act on evidence gained illegally, and we can't wait for them to do it legally."

Ellis and Sheila sat across from Mollie, their brows knit tightly together and eyes flickering nervously around the room.

Sheila gripped her sleeve with her fingertips while Ellis tapped his foot nervously on the floor.

Mollie leaned forward and held Sheila's hand. "We have reason to believe Frank Mathers and his son Jake may have been involved in Henry's death — and the girls' disappearance."

Sheila looked shocked. "Frank?"

Mollie nodded. "It's just a suspicion at this point. That's why we haven't moved in. We need more evidence."

"What evidence do you have so far?" Ellis asked.

Mollie sighed. "Their van matches one seen near where the girls disappeared, lab tests found chemicals on Henry's body consistent with taxidermy supplies, and Jake has a history of gambling debts."

Mollie sat next to Ellis and Sheila, leaned in and whispered. "We think the werewolf angle might be a cover."

Ellis looked up and stared. "Frank has access to animal pelts and wolf fur."

"Don't worry, Ellis. We're getting a warrant, but it takes time."

"Yeah, and meanwhile, my daughter and Linda are God knows where."

"I understand your frustration, Ellis, but if we move too quickly, and they have accomplices, they might hurt the girls."

Ellis stared at Mollie. "If you don't have the warrant soon, I'm going in myself."

"It won't take long."

The shop was dark and closed for the night. Celie and I

approached cautiously from the rear, and peered through a window. "Stay behind me," I whispered.

"Suppose we get caught?"

"We won't," I said, then examined the window. I pushed it up, but it didn't budge, then with strength that surprised me, I pried it open.

I looked back at Celie. "If you hear anything, get help."

"Be careful," Celie said.

I nodded, then climbed through the window into a dark shop.

What the hell am I doing?

The smell of musty, aged leather mixed with a sharp, chemical tang permeated the air.

I sniffed, then sniffed again. Dried moss and old wood led me to a door in the back.

I moved silently through the main room, using my enhanced senses to navigate in the dark. When I reached a door marked employees only, I found it locked.

I applied pressure, then used a nearby crowbar as leverage and broke the lock with a soft click. I hesitated before pushing the door open slowly, cringing with each creak.

The room was cluttered with tools, chemicals, and half-finished projects. I searched methodically, checking drawers and cabinets cluttered with more tools and equipment.

In one drawer, I found a notebook. Opening it, I discovered detailed notes on moon phases, alongside a list of names — including Henry, Amy, and Linda.

I clenched my jaw and balled my fists. *I've got you now, you son of a bitch.*

I continued searching and noticed a slight draft coming from behind a large cabinet. Moving it aside revealed a hidden door, also locked.

I went back to get the crowbar, then used it to break the lock. This time there was no hesitation as I entered the room.

The room was illuminated only by moonlight filtering through a small window. What I saw made me freeze.

The walls were covered with newspaper clippings about missing children from across the region. Photos of young girls were pinned to a board, including recent shots of Amy and Linda that must have been taken after their abduction.

A wolf costume hung on a hook, crafted from real wolf fur with metal claws attached to gloves. Next to it were tranquilizer guns and syringes.

On a desk sat a ledger with names, dates, and dollar amounts. A map on the wall showed locations marked across the country, with one location circled in Los Angeles. It had a calendar next to it with Friday checked, and a time marked beside it: "7:00 PM "

I looked closer, then the ring of a phone startled me, causing me to jump. The answering machine picked up.

"Frank, it's Victor. Everything is ready for Friday night. See you then."

The message ended. I quickly took pictures of everything with my phone, especially the map, then searched the desk.

Suddenly, I heard a car pulling up outside. I listened carefully as I snapped a few more pictures. *Gotta get the hell outta here.*

I quickly exited the hidden room, pushed the cabinet back into place, and headed for the window, slipping out just as the inside door opened.

I heard a car door close outside, then heard the front door of the shop open again — somebody was coming in. I climbed out the same window I entered and found Celie hiding behind a dumpster, watching. I ran over to join her.

She was nervous. "Did you find anything?"

I nodded. "Everything! Let's go."

We slipped away into the darkness before anyone could see us. "We need to go over this," I said.

Chapter Seventeen

ANOTHER NEW PLAN

Once we got home, we sat on the sofa. Celie was more nervous than I'd ever seen her.

I tried to calm her down, then I showed her the photos I'd taken while in Mathers' shop. When she saw the ones of Linda and Amy, she burst into tears.

"Oh, my God, Tulli. He's got them. What are we gonna do?"

She got almost hysterical as she flipped through the photos. "Those claws, and the rest ... They killed Henry. And they took the girls!"

"Not just took them," I said. "They're selling them."

I realized it might upset Celie even more to think of them being trafficked. I squeezed my lips firmly together. "I'm sorry. I didn't mean ..."

Celie shook her head, confused. "We need to tell the police."

I turned to her, more determined than ever to help. "Tell them what? That I broke into Mathers' shop? That I have supernatural senses? What can we tell them?"

"You have proof," she said.

"Illegally obtained proof that no court would accept."

"Then what do we do? We've got to do something."

I made up my mind right then. "We find the girls ourselves. They must be keeping them at the address we saw in Los Angeles."

"We can't just go to LA."

"*I* can. I'll leave tonight."

Celie grabbed hold of my arm. "Not without me."

I shook my head. "You can't. It's too dangerous."

"She's my sister! I'm not staying here while she goes through this."

We stared at each other, and disagreement suddenly turned to understanding.

"Fine," I said. "But we leave now, and we tell no one."

Jake looked around the back room of the taxidermy shop, but when he heard noise, he burst through the kitchen door, finding Frank opening a bottle of Scotch.

"Someone was in the shop!" Jake said.

"What? How do you know?"

"The back window was open. And the cabinet was moved."

Frank set the drink down and ran toward the back. "Did they see inside the room?"

"Things were moved, so I guess whoever was in here, saw everything."

Frank grabbed his keys. "Call Victor. Tell him we're leaving tonight."

"We're driving? That'll take fifteen hours, and that's if we're lucky."

"Then we better start now," Frank said. "This is our retirement. We sell this batch and we're done."

Jones was reviewing evidence when Mollie rushed in. "The state police said the Mathers just left town at a high speed, and they were heading west."

"Did they try to stop them?"

"The sergeant I talked to said they attempted a traffic stop, but the Mathers blew past. Should I tell them to pursue?"

Mollie thought quickly. "No. Let them go, but alert highway patrol and get the warrant now. Emergency basis."

Jones grabbed his phone. "Do you know where they're going?"

"I don't, but I'd bet it's where the girls are."

She dialed Ellis. "Ellis, it's Mollie. The Mathers are on the move and we're getting the warrant now. We think they're heading to wherever they're keeping the girls."

Mollie paused. "And before you ask, you can't go."

"I'm her father, for God's sake."

Mollie paused. "Ellis, I can't be bothered right now. I've got two lunatics who probably kidnapped your girl, and now they're on the run."

She pursed her lips and shook her head. "Sorry. I'm just wondering what the hell spooked the Mathers."

I drove my old pickup with Celie sitting beside me.

"I should call my mom," Celie said.

"Not yet. We don't want anyone following us."

"How far to Los Angeles?"

"About fifteen hours," I said.

Celie shifted in her seat. "Do you think they're still alive?"

"I'd bet on it. These people wouldn't hurt their merchandise." I realized too late what I'd said. "Sorry. I didn't mean to call them merchandise."

I returned my focus on driving, and squinted as the sun shone through the windshield. Nanook's deathbed words rang in my ears as I drove. *Remember, you have both curse and gift. Learn. Be wise.*

"I guess that's one advantage to being a monster," I said.

"I don't know what you're talking about, Tulli, but you're not a monster."

"We'll see."

Mollie called the Los Angeles FBI Office.

"This is Sheriff Mollie Newsom, and I need the district agent. I have a kidnapping and a possible — make that *probable* — trafficking charges against several people."

"Hold on, please."

"I'll hold," Mollie said.

"Give me your number, and Agent Hidalgo will get back to you shortly."

Mollie got with Ellis and Rita. "Okay, you can fly down there and wait. But let me emphasize wait. When the FBI is done, they'll come to you."

I drove for a while, then turned the wheel over to Celie.

Celie drove through the desert while I tried sleeping. She flipped the visor down to block the morning sun. Half a mile later, her phone rang. She looked at the caller ID. "It's my mom," she said.

"You better get it."

After a moment's hesitation, she answered.

"Mom?"

"Celie, it's Sheriff Newsom. Your mother's been worried sick. Where are you?"

"I'm fine, Sheriff. I'm with Tulli."

"With Tulli? What the hell are you doing?"

Celie was hesitant, but determined. "We're going to find Linda."

"Celie, I know you may not listen to me, but your mother said you better get home. And now."

"We know where Linda is, and we're on our way."

Mollie raised her voice. "Celie, get the hell home. The FBI is on their way there."

"We're only a few hours out."

"Pull over right now. If you're with Tulli, you may be in danger."

"I have to go," Celie said. She hung up just as Tulli stared.

"Who was that?"

"The sheriff. She said the FBI is heading to L.A."

"How far behind us?" I asked.

"I don't know. But I know you don't have to do this. It means nothing but trouble for you."

"I know I don't *have* to, but I have to — it's your sister. Besides, the FBI doesn't have time., and these people killed Henry. They won't hesitate to kill the girls if they're cornered."

Celie nodded. "So we keep going?"

"We keep going."

Celie glanced at me as I rubbed sleep from my eyes.

"I never asked — why are you doing this? Is it just for me?"

I yawned, then sat up straight and thought of what Nanook said again. *Always remember, you no hurt innocent people. You have gift and curse. Learn. Be wise.*

I looked at Celie, her face radiant, almost glowing in the morning sun.

"You asked me why I was doing this — I promised my father on his deathbed that I'd never hurt an innocent person. I consider stopping someone from hurting others the same."

I grabbed her hand and squeezed it. "Her being your sister makes it more important."

Chapter Eighteen

THE WAREHOUSE

Los Angeles

Linda and Amy sat on the mattress, looking exhausted and frightened.

The door opened, and Marco entered with Victor Renaldo — sophisticated, and wearing an expensive suit. He looked at the girls and spoke harshly. "Stand up."

The girls complied, trembling.

Victor looked at Marco and gestured to the girls. "Clean them up. Make them presentable for our clients. They arrive at seven tonight."

"Yes, sir."

Victor stood in front of the girls, looking down at them. "Tonight is a very important night. Your futures will be decided by how you are received. If you behave, you'll be treated well. If not ..."

Linda looked up at Victor, her eyes wide and pleading. "Please. Let us go home."

"This is your home now," Victor said, then he laughed and left the room.

Marco approached the girls with fresh clothes. "Shower time."

Amy leaned close to Linda and whispered. "What's going to happen to us?"

Linda squeezed her hand. "Somebody will find us."

Amy teared up. "I don't know how. Nobody even knows where we are."

Los Angeles

I parked my truck in a motel parking lot, then Celie and I moved across the street and climbed a hill. At the top, we peered down at a massive industrial complex.

Metal buildings, with large rust spots showed through coats of gray or beige paint, and the buildings spread for acres. The constant hum of machinery drowned out muffled voices from farther away.

Trucks and trailers were parked nearby and some were backed up to loading docks. Chain-link fences with barbed wire, had security cameras mounted on poles every thirty or forty feet.

"This is it," I said.

"Now what? We need to hurry."

"We wait for it to get as dark as possible, then I go in."

Celie panicked. "We can't wait. We've got to get in there now!"

"Celie, these people have guns."

"You're armed. Kind of."

I looked up at the setting sun. "It's not a full moon, and it won't be for two more nights. Right now, I'm just a man, maybe with a slight edge."

"You're still stronger than normal, right?"

"But not bulletproof."

As we talked, my phone rang. Caller ID showed "Unknown Number."

"Tulli, it's Mollie."

The call took me by surprise. "Sheriff, how did you —"

"I tracked your cell, and I know you're in LA." There was a pause, then she started up again. "Listen to me very carefully. Do *not* approach that building. We have a tactical team forty minutes out. I don't want you getting hurt."

"I appreciate your concern, Sheriff. But we don't have forty minutes; they're selling the girls at seven o'clock."

"How do you know that?"

"I just know."

"Stay put, Tulli. That's an order. These men are dangerous."

"I understand, Sheriff. But the last I knew, I didn't work for you," I said, then hung up.

"The police are coming?" Celie asked.

"Mollie said in forty minutes, but the auction starts at seven." I looked at my phone. "And it's six fifty-five now. We can't wait."

I handed Celie my phone. "Hang onto this. I won't need it." Then I reached into my pocket and pulled out the silver necklace Nanook had given me. I handed that to Celie. "If anything happens, put this around my neck. It will keep me from changing. I don't want people to see me as that creature."

Celie leaned over and kissed me. "What are you going to do?"

"What I have to."

"But it's not a full moon. You wont have any powers."

"I have to do something. Your sister is in there. Other little girls are in there too."

I then moved down the hill toward the fence. I rubbed the amulet that had become a permanent fixture around my neck. *Help me do the right thing, Ataata.*

I felt my eyes change. They must have flashed yellow in the gathering darkness.

Victor addressed a small crowd of people, most dressed in suits. "Gentlemen, thank you for your patience. Tonight we have some exceptional merchandise. Young, healthy, and ... compliant. I guarantee you will be satisfied."

Victor leaned forward, his voice low and cold. "I've sampled them myself."

Marco stood guard by the door to the small room where the girls were kept.

Jake Mathers nervously paced behind the stage, while Frank watched from the shadows.

"We'll begin with a special item. Straight from the heartland. Untouched, and pure."

He signaled to Marco, who entered the back room.

Chapter Nineteen

THE AUCTION

Los Angeles

I scaled the side of the building with agility that I didn't think I'd have without a full moon. After going a few steps, I found a roof-top skylight. Looking down, I saw the auction setup and the men waiting. I tensed when the auctioneer banged his gavel.

My face contorted with rage, as I looked for a way in, then I spotted a large ventilation duct and pried it open.

I crawled through the narrow space and followed the sounds of voices from below. I saw the auction taking place through a grate in the ductwork.

Through another grate, I spotted the small room where several children were being held, including Linda and Amy.

My nails extended into claws. I stared at my hands, shock register-ing. *I don't know how this is happening, but I'm damn glad it is. But* why *am I changing? It's not a full moon. What if I lose control? What about the girls?*

I hesitated, but the sound of a young girl crying brought back memories of my promise: *You have gift and curse.*

Those memories spurred me on.

The change began slowly, my skin rippled and veins darkened. Fur sprouted from what seemed like every pore in my body. My fingers and knuckles grew bigger.

My bones creaked, and when my jaw thrust forward, the bones sounded as if they'd break. My nose flattened and my nostrils flared. Muscles swelled beneath my skin, making my body into a wild, primal form.

My eyes changed last, becoming amber, and almost glowing with an eerie light. The beast that I turned into stared ahead, then a deep guttural growl filled the room.

Marco returned, leading Amy onto the stage. She looked terrified, dressed in a white dress, her face blank with fear.

Victor took center stage. "Let's start the bidding at fifty thousand."

Hands raised across the room.

Agent Hidalgo and several SWAT team members approached the warehouse.

Hidalgo spoke quietly into the radio. "Team One, are you in position?"

"Affirmative. Rear entrance covered."

Hidalgo paused to make sure no one was around, then spoke again. "Team two?"

"Side entrance secured. Awaiting your order."

Hidalgo checked his weapon. "We go on my mark."

Celie waited anxiously by my truck. She spotted the police vehicles when they pulled up and ran toward them.

"Officer!"

Agent Hidalgo looked around, then back to Celie. He appeared shocked. "Where did you come from?"

"I'm with Tulli, and he's inside."

Hidalgo shook his head and sighed. "All units, we have a civilian inside. Accelerate timeline but be careful." Hidalgo checked his watch, then pressed the radio intercom. "All units, go. Go now!"

Back on the roof, I looked through the skylight as the bidding for Amy continued.

Victor ran the show, standing on a stage, holding a microphone. "I have seventy-five thousand. Do I hear eighty?"

More hands raised. Amy stood on the stage trembling, tears streaming down her face.

The audience looked on as the bidding continues. The crashing sound of glass shattering drew their attention upward.

I dropped down onto a catwalk above the auction floor.

I had transformed now — my eyes glowed yellow, and my teeth elongated into fangs, nails extended into claws. My muscles bulged beneath his shirt, and my movements were fluid, almost predatory. Nanook's words came to me again. *Do not hurt anyone. Do not kill.*

Victor reeled back in shock. "What the hell!"

Men rose from their seats in confusion. Marco drew a gun and fired at me, but I dodged with speed I shouldn't have had.

I leapt across the stage, landing between Amy and Victor. He grabbed Amy and pushed her toward the exit.

I chased after Victor, and when he turned to look at me, I shouted to Amy. "Run!" My voice was more of a growl than human.

Victor pulled a gun, but I got to him before he could pull the trigger and swatted it away with a powerful blow to his side.

Jake was on the side of the stage. He panicked and raced toward the back room. He yelled as he opened the door. "Move the other merchandise, now"

Jake burst in and grabbed Linda roughly. "We're leaving."

Linda yanked away and ran, but she had nowhere to go. "I'm not going anywhere with you."

The door crashed in, hitting Jake. I ran into the room, now fully transformed despite the lack of a full moon. *The stress and rage must have accelerated the changing.*

"Linda, get behind me."

Linda screamed. "Who are you? *What* are you?"

"A friend," I said.

Jake recovered, pulling a knife. He lunged at me, but I caught his arm and twisted. The knife clattered to the floor as Jake howled in pain. "Don't kill me. Please?"

I stood over top of Jake and stared. "Where's Frank?"

Jake hesitated, until I placed my foot on his neck. "Main floor," he said.

Chapter Twenty

RESCUE

SWAT teams breached all entrances simultaneously as gunfire erupted from inside.

Chaos reigned. Clients scattered, some being apprehended by police. Marco ran, all the while, he exchanged gunfire with officers from behind cover.

Victor grabbed Amy, using her as a shield as he backed up. "Stay back or she dies!"

Police officers held their positions, weapons trained on Victor.

Frank hid behind some crates and looked for an escape route.

Tulli led Linda and the other children down a hallway. Gunfire sounded all around them.

Linda looked up at me. It was clear she was frightened. "What's happening?"

I checked the halls. "We need another way out."

I sniffed the air, then pointed to a side corridor. "This way."

We turned just as Frank appeared at the other end of the hallway, wielding a shotgun. "Stop right there."

I pushed the children to safety around the corner just as Frank fired. "Stay here."

Linda grabbed hold of my wrist and squeezed. "Don't leave us! Please?"

I looked her in the eyes. "I'll be right back."

I stepped into the hallway, facing Frank.

He stepped back when he saw me. "What the hell are you?"

When I answered him, it came out as a guttural growl. "The monster you've been pretending to be."

Frank fired again. The shot grazed my arm, but I barely flinched. Then I charged forward with incredible speed.

Frank tried to reload, but I reached him first, knocking the shotgun away. I lifted Frank by the throat and pinned him against the wall. "You killed Henry," I said, and squeezed his throat harder. "You took those girls."

Frank choked and gasped for breath. "Please?"

My fangs extended further, my control slipping. "Give me one reason not to tear your throat out."

Frank stammered. "I can help save the others. I know where Victor keeps them."

I hesitated, fighting with my instincts to rip him apart. *I promise, Ataa. I promise.* "Where?"

"Basement level. Hidden room. Code is 3-9-7-1."

I released Frank, who collapsed to the floor, gasping. "If you're lying ..."

"I'm not. I swear."

I turned back toward Linda, but as I did, Frank pulled a hidden pistol from his ankle holster. "Die, you freak."

Frank fired. The bullet struck me in the back. I stumbled but didn't fall. Instead, I turned slowly, my face contorted with rage.

"Wrong choice," I said, my voice sounding like an inhuman growl.

Frank fired again, but I was already moving too fast to track. I struck him with one powerful blow, knocking him unconscious rather than killing him. *I'm not the monster. You are.*

Victor continued backing toward an exit, using Amy as a shield. "Anyone follows me, she dies."

Suddenly, the lights went out, plunging the warehouse into darkness. In the confusion, something fast and powerful knocked Victor's legs out from under him. He fell, losing his grip on Amy and giving her the chance to scramble away just as police tactical units cut through the darkness. They found Victor on the ground, disarmed and looking terrified.

"What the hell was that?" Victor asked.

Amy ran straight to Agent Hidalgo. She hugged him and cried, then suddenly turned, looking around. "Where's Linda?"

Agent Hidalgo patted her back. "We're still looking for her."

Amy looked up at Hidalgo. "The wolfman was helping her."

"Wolfman?"

Amy nodded. "He saved us from the bad man. He jumped from up there." She pointed to the broken skylight.

Agent Hidalgo looked up and shook his head. "From up there?"

Amy nodded again.

Bleeding but determined to get these girls to safety, I led them down a dark corridor, step by step, cautioning them to remain quiet. I stopped at a door with a keypad, then punched in the code Jake had given me: 3-9-7-1.

The door clicked open, revealing several more terrified children. Some of them backed up, apparently afraid of what they saw, but Linda assured them things were fine. "We're getting you out of here," I said.

Linda looked at the wound where the bullet struck me. "You're hurt."

"Just keep moving," I said.

They headed toward a stairwell, and my transformation began to reverse as my strength waned.

Linda looked closely at me. "Tulli?"

"Shh."

I felt my eyes flicker, then Linda whispered to me. "Your eyes are yellow."

"I know, just keep going," I said.

At the top of the stairs, they encountered SWAT officers.

"Freeze!" an officer shouted.

Linda jumped in front of me and spread her arms. "Don't shoot. He saved us."

The officers looked at each other and assessed the situation. After a long moment's hesitation, the SWAT team lowered their weapons slightly, confused by my appearance and Linda's report.

My voice had returned to normal now. I looked up at an officer. "Take them to safety," I said, then slumped against the wall, the bullet wound apparently taking its toll.

Two officers moved in to help me stand and assisted me down the corridor. One of them got on the radio "We need medical. Civilian down."

"Don't let him die," Linda said. "Please?"

Agent Hidalgo rounded the corner, several officers, and Amy, following him.

"Linda!" Amy shouted.

Linda broke free and ran to Amy. They hugged and cried, and ended up laughing.

"Amy! Oh my God! We made it. " They hugged more, and cried more.

"All right, let's get you girls to your mothers. They're right across the street," Agent Hidalgo said.

As they walked over, Hidalgo called Ellis. "I'm on my way. We've got both girls, and they're safe."

THE RETURN

Hidalgo parks and the girls jump out and run to their mothers.

Linda opens her arms and runs to Rita. "Mom!"

Almost at the same time, Amy ran to her mom and dad. "Mom, Dad!"

Rita knelt down in the parking lot. "Thank God, you're safe. Thank God." Tears streamed down her face.

Ellis and Sheila hugged Amy, and held her tightly. "My baby. My baby," Sheila said.

Hidalgo waited until the girls' parents had them secured, then he headed back to the warehouse.

Ambulances and police vehicles filled the street, then news vans arrived, and reporters set up to film.

Paramedics loaded me into an ambulance as Celie pushed through the crowd.

"Tulli!."

The paramedic stopped her. "Are you family?"

"I'm all he has," Celie said.

The paramedic looked to his partner, then nodded, letting her climb in.

Celie held my hands and kissed my cheek. "Stay with me, please?"

My voice was barely audible, but I managed to whisper. "Don't forget to put the necklace on me. I don't want to change."

The ambulance drove off carrying me and Celie.

Agent Hidalgo looked around, surveilling the scene, then he drove back to the motel.

Rita held Linda tightly, refusing to let her go.

Linda looked up at her. "He saved us, Mom."

"I know dear. Agent Hidalgo is a brave man."

Linda pulled away and looked up. "Not him, Mom. The wolfman."

Rita looked down at her, eyebrows raised. "What are you talking about?"

Ellis pulled Rita aside and whispered. "Amy said the same thing. She said there was a wolfman in there that set them free. It might be best if we didn't say anything."

Agent Hidalgo approached. "All the children are accounted for. Seven in total, including Amy and Linda."

"And the men responsible?" Ellis asked.

"All in custody. Victor Renaldo, Frank and Jake Mathers, Marco Diaz, and six others. We've also arrested twelve of their so called clients."

"I hope they rot in prison."

Agent Hidalgo knelt next to Amy and spoke calmly. "Back in the warehouse, you mentioned a wolfman."

Amy moved behind her father's back.

Ellis spoke to protect her. "Probably a police officer in tactical gear. The mind plays tricks in traumatic situations."

Hidalgo looked at Amy, then Ellis. "Probably."

Rita looked around, almost panicking. "What about Celie?"

Agent Hidalgo responded. "She rode in the ambulance with the young man who was shot."

Hidalgo shook his head. "Strange about him. The officer who found him said he saw some unusual markings on him, but when he got to him, they were gone."

Ellis looked worried. "What do you mean?"

"Nothing. Just unusual."

I opened my eyes and realized I was in a hospital bed, hooked to an assortment of tubes and connected to several monitors. Celie sat next to me holding my hand.

A knock at the door revealed Mollie. "Mind if I come in?"

"I'll give you privacy," Celie said. Before leaving, she handed me a small box with my silver bracelet inside. The burning sensation on my neck told me she'd had it on me the night before.

"What are you doing here, Sheriff?"

Mollie smiled. "I took the first flight I could get. I wasn't gonna let the town hero be stuck down here all alone, though I should have known Celie would be with you."

Mollie took the seat where Celie had been. "The doctors say you're recovering remarkably fast."

"Good genes, I guess."

"Must be," Mollie said.

She placed a small object on the bedside table. "The doctor removed this from your back. I thought you might want it."

I was cautious in how I answered. "Why would I want a bullet?"

"Call it a memento of what you did for those children."

"I just helped the police."

Mollie leaned closer. "Several witnesses described something ... unusual helping them. Something fast, strong. Something with yellow eyes."

I shook my head and tried to smile. "Must have been stress. Those girls went through a lot."

Mollie nodded. "That they did." She stood to leave, then turned back. "You know, Tulli, whoever, or whatever, saved those children deserves my gratitude — hell, the whole town's gratitude. When you see them, thank them for me."

Mollie walked to the door, then looked back. "Oh, and Tulli, that bullet's silver."

When she left, I stared at the bullet. *She knows.*

Chapter Twenty-Two

BACK HOME

The courtroom was packed for the sentencing of Frank and Jake Mathers as the judge delivered the verdict.

The judge banged his gavel and spoke. "Frank Mathers, for the murder of Henry Litkin and your role in the abduction and trafficking of minors, this court sentences you to life imprisonment without the possibility of parole."

Frank hung his head as the judge continued.

"Jake Mathers, for your role in abducting and trafficking minors, this court sentences you to forty years imprisonment."

Ellis sat with his family, watching grimly. The Mattsons sat behind them, and I sat beside Celie.

As we exited the courtroom, Little Hawk approached. "I was wrong about you, Tulli. And wrong about the werewolf."

I nodded. "Sometimes men are the real monsters, Little Hawk"

"I've heard stories that something was in the warehouse that night. Something that saved the girls."

"I can't imagine what."

Little Hawk shrugged. "The Great Spirit often looks out for the innocent. I guess this time he did good."

Linda sat at the kitchen table, drawing as Rita watched from the doorway, concerned but relieved to have her daughter back. "What are you drawing, honey?"

Linda held up a picture of a werewolf fighting bad men. "The wolfman who saved us."

"Sweetheart, the doctors said that might have been your imagination. A police officer in special gear, maybe."

Linda continued drawing, but spoke confidently. "He was real. And he was good, even though he looked scary."

Rita kissed Linda's head. "I'm just glad you're home."

Mollie sat at her desk, reviewing reports when Jones entered with coffee. "Still working?"

"Just finishing up. The Mathers' case is officially closed."

"Good. This town needs to heal."

Mollie closed her laptop and looked at Jones. "Do you ever wonder if there are things out there we don't understand?"

"You mean like werewolves?"

Mollie stared at Jones for a moment. "Maybe." She motioned for Jones to sit.

"When the town went wild with werewolf theories, I researched a few accounts of them in Europe. I even called a police captain." When Jones said nothing, Mollie continued. "What they told me ... let's just say, it made me more of a believer in Little Hawk's tales."

Mollie paused again. "But to answer my own question, yes, I think there's plenty in this world we don't understand. And sometimes, that's okay."

"I guess," Jones said. "Anyway, it's time to go back to boring work where I don't have to worry about things like that."

Mollie laughed as she left, then Jones opened his drawer.

Inside was a plaster cast of an unusual footprint — neither fully human nor animal. He studied it thoughtfully, then closed the drawer, nodding as he did. *Sometimes, that's okay.*

On Main Street, children played volleyball, swam in the nearby pond, and even took romps in the woods. Adults sat and chatted, enjoying the weather.

Amy and Linda sat on a bench, eating ice cream when Celie and I walked by, holding hands.

The girls waved, and I waved back, sharing a secret smile with them. Then the girls ran up to me and give me a hug.

Linda winked at me. "I'm not afraid anymore."

"Me neither," Amy said.

I tousled their hair, then Celie and I walked off together, almost bumping into Rita on the narrow walk.

Rita seemed friendlier than normal. "I should have known I'd find you two together."

I laughed, relieved that there seemed to be no suspicions. "I just saw Linda. How's she doing?"

"She still sees a psychiatrist twice a week. Dr. Winters says it'll take time. But she seems to be doing well. Both her and Amy."

"That's good to hear," I said.

Rita seemed to study me for a moment, then said. "You know, she still talks about you helping her. And about ... the wolfman, as she calls him."

I shifted uncomfortably. "Kids have big imaginations."

"They do, but sometimes they see things more clearly than adults." Rita gulped. "All I know is whatever happened in that warehouse ... whoever helped save my daughter, I'm grateful."

"I'm just glad they're safe."

"Me too," Rita said, then she looked at me and smiled. "Tulli, would you like to come to dinner again? I guarantee it will be more pleasant."

She then looked at Celie. "I'm sure Celie wouldn't mind. And I think Linda would like it too."

I glanced at Celie, then back to Rita. "I'd like that. Thanks."

"Plan on next week sometime. Make it convenient for yourself." Rita walked off to get Linda and Amy.

"Wow, that was unexpected," Celie said.

I smiled and continued the walk with Celie.

My father told me our kind was cursed, but we were also gifted. Maybe it is a gift — if we use it right.

As we walked away, we saw the kids playing, and heard them laughing. It forced a smile on our faces.

Every monster has a choice. To embrace the darkness or to fight for the light. I've made mine.

Above the town, barely visible in the daylight sky, the faint outline of a full moon could be seen.

～

Celie knocked on my door, then entered. She glanced around, and smiled. "I see you unpacked your bags. Thinking of staying?"

I grabbed her and kissed her passionately. "Thanks to someone special, I believe I will."

I stepped back a moment, then looked in her eyes. "I've been thinking about our future. Maybe we could adopt. If we do that, it breaks the curse."

Celie's eyes gleamed. "I don't think so."

My head drooped. "Oh ... Well, I didn't expect you to ... We don't have to have kids."

Celie laughed. "No, you ass. I meant that I don't think we'll adopt. I want to have our own kids."

"But ..."

"But nothing. We'll teach them to learn control. You and me."

I kissed her again, then grabbed her arm and led her outside. The full moon was almost visible.

I prepared for transformation in a clearing near the cabin. The full moon rose above.

Celie sat nearby on a fallen log. "Are you sure about this?"

"The cell isn't necessary anymore. I can control it now."

"Because of what happened in L.A.?"

"Partly. My father's words were always with me, but I think saving those children helped me understand what I am. What I can be."

"Which is?"

"Something in between. Not just a monster, not just a man."

The transformation began. But unlike before, it was less painful, more controlled. My body shifted and changed, fur sprouting, limbs elongating. My eyes glowed yellow, but they retained their humanity.

The transformation complete, the werewolf that was Tulli sat calmly beside Celie. She reached out, tentatively touching my fur, and I made a sound, almost like a purr.

"So what now?"

I looked up at the moon, then back at Celie. I rose and offered my clawed hand to her. She took it, unafraid, then leaned over and kissed my cheek.

"A moonlight walk it is, then."

We walked together into the forest, an unlikely pair under the full moon — the woman and the werewolf.

ACKNOWLEDGMENTS

It is with great honor that I give eternal gratitude to my wife, Mikki. My four grandkids: Joey, Dante, Adalina, and Carmine. And my great grandson, Enzo. They give me the inspiration to keep going.

ABOUT THE AUTHOR

Giacomo Giammatteo is the author of gritty crime dramas about murder, mystery, and family. He also writes nonfiction books, including the No Mistakes Careers, No Mistakes Publishing, No Mistakes Grammar, and No Mistakes Writing series.

When Giacomo isn't writing, he's helping his wife take care of the animals in their sanctuary. At last count, they had forty-five — eleven dogs, one horse, six cats, and twenty-six pigs.

Oh, and one crazy — and very large — wild boar, who takes walks with Giacomo every day and also happens to be his best buddy.

nomistakespublishing.com
gg@giacomog.com

ALSO BY GIACOMO GIAMMATTEO

And you can buy them on the platform of your choice.

This brings up a thought: With more than eighty books out now, it is becoming difficult to try to update the list at the back of all of them. If you want to know what books I have out, use the link above, which takes you to my website, or download the latest copy of my GG recommended reading list, which is free.

Nonfiction

Careers

No Mistakes Resumes, Book I of No Mistakes Careers

No Mistakes Interviews, Book II of No Mistakes Careers

Grammar

Misused Words, No Mistakes Grammar, Volume I

Misused Words for Business, No Mistakes Grammar, Volume II

More Misused Words, No Mistakes Grammar, Volume III

Visual Grammar (This is a compilation of volumes I–III with a bit of new information added. It also includes pictures and is the world's first visual grammar book)

Misused Words and Then Some, No Mistakes Grammar, Volume V

Simply Put: The Plain English Grammar Guide

How to Capitalize Anything

More Grammar

No Mistakes Grammar Bites, Volume I: Lie, Lay, Laid, and It's and Its

No Mistakes Grammar Bites, Volume II: Good and Well, and Then and Than

No Mistakes Grammar Bites, Volume III: That, Which, and Who, and There Is and There Are

No Mistakes Grammar Bites, Volume IV: Affect and Effect, and Accept and Except

No Mistakes Grammar Bites, Volume V: You're and Your, and They're, There, and Their

No Mistakes Grammar Bites, Volume VI: Passed and Past, and Into, In to and In

No Mistakes Grammar Bites, Volume VII: Farther and Further, and Onto, On, and On To

No Mistakes Grammar Bites, Volume VIII: Anxious and Eager, and Different From and Different Than

No Mistakes Grammar Bites, Volume IX, A While and Awhile, and Envy and Jealousy

No Mistakes Grammar Bites, Volume X, Could've and Should've, and Irony and Coincidence

No Mistakes Grammar Bites, Volume XI: "Quotation Marks and How to Punctuate Them" and "Plurals of Compound Nouns"

No Mistakes Grammar Bites, Volume XII: "Latin Abbreviations"

No Mistakes Grammar Bites, Volume XIII: "Redundancies" and "Ax to Grind"

No Mistakes Grammar Bites Volume XIV: "Superlatives and How We Use them Wrong"

No Mistakes Grammar Bites Volume XV: "Shoo-in and Shoe-in" and "Horse Racing Sayings"

No Mistakes Grammar Bites Volume XVI: "Which and What" and "Since and Because"

No Mistakes Grammar Bites Volume XVII: "Hyphens, and When to Use Them" and "Em Dashes and En Dashes"

No Mistakes Grammar Bites Volume XVIII: "Words Difficult to Pronounce" and "Could Not Care Less"

No Mistakes Grammar Bites Volume XIX, "Punctuation" and "When You Don't Need the Word Personal"

No Mistakes Grammar Bites, Volume XX, "When Is Currently Needed?" And "Intervene and Interfere"

No Mistakes Grammar Bites, Volume XXI: "More Hyphen Questions" and Myself, Me, Themselves and Themselves."

No Mistakes Grammar Bites, Volume XXII: "Words You May Be Using Wrong, Part One"

Murder Is Immaculate (coming soon)

Blood Flows South Series

A Bullet for Carlos: A Connie Gianelli Mystery

Finding Family, a Novella

A Bullet from Dominic

The Good Book

The Ranger

Redemption Series

Necessary Decisions: A Gino Cataldi Mystery

Old Wounds

Promises Kept, the Story of Number Two

Premeditated

The Ranger

Rules of Vengeance Series (Fantasy)

Light of Lights (the beginning, a novella)

A Promise of Vengeance

Undeniable Vengeance

Consummate Vengeance

Vengeance Is Mine (2019)

Note: *Light of Lights* is a novella. It's about 100 pages long and sets the stage for the series. The other books in the series are between 650 and 850 pages long.

Other Books

You can always see current and upcoming books on my website.

Fiction

Memories for Sale (mystery/sf)

The Joshua Citadel (SF novella)

Children's Books

No Mistakes Grammar for Kids, Volume I: Much and Many

No Mistakes Grammar for Kids, Volume II: Lie and Lay

No Mistakes Grammar for Kids, Volume III: Bring and Take

No Mistakes Grammar for Kids, Volume IV: "Would've, Should've" and "Your and You're"

No Mistakes Grammar for Kids, Volume V: "There, They're, and Their" and "To, Too, and Two"

Shinobi Goes to School—Life on the Farm for Kids, Volume I

Fiona Gets Caught, Life on the Farm for Kids, Volume II

Coco Gets a Donut, Life on the Farm for Kids, Volume III

Squeak Gets a Home, Life on the Farm for Kids, Volume IV

Biscotti Saves Punch, Life on the Farm for Kids, Volume V

The Adventures of Adalina, Volume I: Adalina and the Five Tiny Bears

Coming Soon

The Adventures of Adalina, Volume II: Adalina and the Underwater Bears

Get on the mailing list, and you'll be notified of release dates and sales.

And don't forget to leave a review!

Mailing list

www.ingramcontent.com/pod-product-compliance
Lightning Source LLC
Chambersburg PA
CBHW021248200726

48288CB00015B/3051